AT THE EDGE
OF THE ~~UNIVERSE~~

On a small planetoid at the furthest edge of space lives Space Warden Seth Paradine, surrounded by an artificial environment designed to resemble Earth. But the placid routine of this unusual outpost is shattered by three intruders—a millionaire tycoon, his arrogant young assistant, and his beautiful, coldly neurotic daughter.

Paradine warns them of the dangers of no-space, where literally anything is possible, and nothing certain—not even death. But the four are soon lost—plunged into unimaginable chaos through THE HOLE IN THE ZERO.

the hole in the zero

m.k. joseph

I go and I return: I would I were
The pilot of the darkness and the dream

AN AVON BOOK

ONE

THE HOUSE WAS low and sprawling, built of grey stone, shaded by a steep roof of golden thatch. The leaded panes of the bow-windows gleamed warmly in the westering sun. In the front garden, crazy-paving wandered among beds banked high with old-fashioned flowers, pink and mignonette, pansy and geranium, foxglove and hollyhock. They wavered gently in the afternoon breeze, which carried a scent of honeysuckle and the murmur of innumerable bees and the moan of doves. Beehives could be seen among the banked flowers, and nine bean-rows, and a sundial.

Beyond the tall hedgerow, clipped into topiary shapes of birds, the air over the meadow shimmered with heat haze. A gong began to beat on two notes. The shimmer flickered faster and faster into an eye-aching blur, and at the same time a red glow shifted up and away into the ultra-violet. There was a soft explosion of air which rocked the old-fashioned flowers in the garden, and the tall lop-sided shape of a Kraag mark ten deep-space runabout slid down the anti-gravity beam and seemed to materialize lightly upon the grass of the meadow. The gong-beat fell silent.

The wicket gate clicked shut behind the three passengers. First the thickset man, with a huge body and completely bald head, who walked everywhere as if he owned the place, because he often did; then the very handsome girl with the crazy blue eyes; last, the young albino in the beautiful clothes. The girl stopped by the sundial, tapping the old gnomon with her gold fingershield so that it rang faintly.

"What is it?" she said without curiosity.

"Some neolithic thing for telling the time—sun and shadow," said the young man.

5

"It's insane," she said. "Insane and beautiful. Buy me one."

The thickset man remained for a moment staring at the dial, as if expecting to see the shadow move, and then glanced at the tiny sidereal chronometer strapped to his wrist. He shrugged his huge shoulders and followed the others to the house.

The girl tapped her foot on the "Welcome" mat, sniffed the honeysuckle, listened to the bees and doves. "Insane," she murmured, "quite insane and beautiful. You know."

The young man touched the brass lion's-head knocker, and almost at once the door creaked open. The old white-headed butler stood bowing gently before them.

"Oh, *good* h'afternoon, sir—*good* h'afternoon, miss— and young sir. You're *most* welcome, h'I'm sure. I'm *Smithers*, sir. The *master's* waiting for you in the parlour. *This* way, *h'if* you please—and *do* mind your 'eads on the low beams, gentlemen."

As the old oak door creaked shut behind them, the breeze ceased to blow in the garden, and honeysuckle no longer scented the air. The bees stopped murmuring and the doves stopped moaning. The afternoon sun went out.

What the butler had called the parlour was a long low room which glowed gently with dark polished oak and old Brussels carpets. A huge log fire blazed on iron trivets in the open hearth. There were shelves of old leather-bound books, and an open sideboard set with Wedgwood and Delftware, and a tall grandfather clock which ticked mellowly.

The dark young man who rose to greet them from the smoking chair by the fire seemed slight, but only because he was well-proportioned and wore the trim khaki uniform of a Limitary Warden—a proud uniform which carried neither medals nor badges of rank. At his full height, he stood equal with the thickset man, and overtopped the others.

"Good afternoon, Mr. Kraag," he said. "Welcome to station Gamma Seventeen. I've been expecting you

6

since we got the priority clearance from local base. I'm Seth Paradine."

"Glad to know you, Warden Paradine," rumbled the big man. "Permit me to present you to my daughter, Miss Helena."

"I'm honoured by your presence here, Miss Helena."

"You're sweet," she said, and her blue eyes swept restlessly across his dark face and about the softly glowing room. "Isn't it all just sweet? You know."

"And this is Miss Helena's contracted fiancé, my official heir-executive, Hyperion Merganser."

The beautifully dressed young man grinned. "Everyone calls me Bill," he said. "Hi, brother."

"My cordial respects, Mr. Merganser," said Paradine with propriety.

"Won't you ever learn to follow protocol?" muttered Kraag angrily to his heir-executive.

"I'd rather sit on my dignity than stand on it," said Merganser, "or so the birdies say." And he eased himself into one of the leather armchairs without waiting for the others.

"Please sit down," said Paradine quickly, covering the awkwardness. "Mr. Kraag, please try this grandfather-chair, it's really most comfortable. Miss Helena, you might be interested in this rocker—it's an authentic Kennedy replica. Now if you'll allow me I'll ring for tea."

He pulled a brass lever beside the fireplace, and a bell tinkled far away. The afternoon glow seemed to be fading in the room. It was only when the blazing light of the fire caught his dark young face that the others could begin to see the tight lines of strain.

"You had a good journey, I hope?"

"Smooth as a pint of gin," said Merganser. "No fuzz. Why doubt it? They're all the same."

"So it ought to've been," growled Kraag. "We've got the new mark ten, duplicate overdrive, chrono-stabilization, the boxful—*and* a complete set of Heisenberg shields. The trip's costing me the equivalent of six months gross product of a whole planet. A rich planet," he added.

7

"Grief of stars," said Paradine softly, with awe. "You fitted Heisenbergs to a ship *that* big?"

"We couldn't all get into one of your little runabouts," said Kraag.

Paradine sat up stiffly. "Are you telling me, Mr. Kraag, that you all plan on going—back there?" He gestured towards the back of the house.

"We are and we shall," said Kraag. "I've got a very special open licence from the Authority. Had to go right up to Number Two to get it." He chuckled. "That's included in the price tag too."

"But Mr. Kraag, you ought to know—"

"We'll discuss it later," said Kraag, "not that it matters."

Miss Helena was rocking gently to and fro, in time with the ticking of the old clock. "I spent most of the trip in the dreambox," she said, "but I had bad dreams you know, really paralysing ones."

"It's time you let me take charge of your dreams, dolly," said Merganser.

"You were in them," she said abruptly, staring at the clock.

Kraag leaned over towards Paradine. "You understand, Warden," he muttered, "my daughter needed a rest. That's why I arranged this trip for her."

There was a discreet tap at the door, and the old butler entered wheeling an immense tea-trolley, the various decks of which were loaded with steaming urns and spirit kettles, silver teapots and cream jugs, cakestands, muffincovers and trays of sandwiches.

"Begging your pardon, sirs and miss," said the old man, "what may I pour for you? Miss? India, Ceylon or China?"

"China."

"Cream, milk or lemon, miss?"

"Cream."

The old butler winced faintly.

"China—lemon," said Kraag.

"I'll have coffee," said Merganser.

"Certainly, sir, Brazilian, Mexican, or Turkish, sir?"

"Please yourself, little brother. Just see it's got brandy in it."

8

"As you wish, sir. French, Cape, or Australian, sir?"

After the old man had served them, and uncovered the dishes of muffins and scones, and recommended the iced madeira cake for which Cook was especially renowned, he doddered off to light the lamps under their broad shades of patterned glass. From a dark corner an old bassett-hound crept out, and laid its muzzle on Paradine's knee; thumping its tail on the floor, it gazed up at him with rheumy eyes.

"He's sweet," said the girl. "Is he real?"

Paradine looked distressed. There was a moment's silence and Merganser said:

"Shouldn't ask that one, dolly. A dog's a dog. Let it be."

"But I want to know," said the girl, in a hard shrill voice.

"Well," said Paradine sadly, "factually no. He's a robot, like all the rest. I suppose you've guessed. All this—" he waved a hand around "—the synthesiser came on the first ship. It dug itself in as soon as I landed, and made its own extensions. It can make anything I need—fresh flowers, old port, fuel, haplodisers—anything. Except robots. They have to be assembled at base, because we can't programme the Huxley units here. It costs a lot to get them here too."

"Your butler?" said Merganser.

"And the rest," said Paradine, "they're all one unit actually, with changeable cladding and a repertory of character tapes. It's a very versatile unit."

"Sounds like one of our K59 Superfactotum models," said Kraag with satisfaction.

"That's right, Mr. Kraag. I'm very fond of it really. It can do Mrs. Wiggins the lovable old housekeeper, and Pat the drunken Irish gardner, and Bert the shrewd cockney handyman, and Taffy the Welsh synthotech, and Ron the Australian bush pilot—that's when he doubles as auxiliary computer on the ship."

"So it's all fake," said the girl sulkily, staring into the fire. "Boss Kraag, you've brought me across a crillion miles of bad dreams and empty space to see a lot of oldy fakes."

9

"Not fake," said Paradine in the same sad even voice, "make-believe."

"Fake."

"Sweetheart, there's reasons," said Kraag, looking up at Paradine, who had risen from his chair. He picked up one of the lamps, and held it up to the wall above the roll top desk. Two framed samplers hung there, carefully crewel-stitched in coloured wools, with ornamental borders of old-fashioned flowers, like those in the garden outside. One of them said: CHAOS IS HELL.

The other said: HELL IS DULL.

"And that's really the truth of it," said Paradine, setting down the lamp.

"Back homeside, everyone thinks that you Wardens have the glamourest job in the cosmos," said Merganser. "It's always on the video. The thing, you know—space dragons, diamond planets, super-dollies, the fires of longevity—all that kind of carousel."

"Oh that," said the Warden, "that's for the funnies. On the old maps, Earthside, when they didn't know what there was there, they put Here Be Dragons. It's nothing like that at all."

"Tell me the news," said the girl, leaning forward, suddenly intent. "What is it like? I want to know—what is it like?"

"It's like—" Paradine spread his hands inarticulately "—it's like—nothing."

"You mean, just empty space?" said Kraag. "It seems I've come a long way and spent a lot of money for nothing."

"No, it's not that," Paradine shook his dark head violently. "Don't expect that—if you do it'll scare you dreary. If you must go, at least try to understand. It's like nothing you can expect, but try. Look," he said slowly "even empty space is full of something—four dimensions, physical laws, causation, potentiality. But back there it's all gone."

"No space?"

"Not that either. Take away what you think of—it's not there—no probability, no possibility. So anything is probable, anything is possible. No time—all time. No space—any space. Nothing—everything."

Kraag's chair creaked as he shrugged his massive shoulders. "I didn't make a crillion solars by having an imagination. You'll just have to show me, Warden."

"I can't refuse an Authority clearance, Mr. Kraag," said Paradine in a level voice. "But it's your risk, your very own risk."

"I've never passed up a safe risk," said Kraag. "My tame geniuses assure me that the ship is one hundred percent safe."

"It's not the ship, it's the mind," said Paradine.

"I don't think young Billy's liking this," said Bill Merganser. "What about you, doll?"

But the girl was leaning back in the rocker, staring at the two inscriptions.

"Of course, the Heisenbergs screen out the worst of it, and the scanners do a certain amount of interpretation. And we've got conditioning," said Paradine. "We have to take it even before entering the observatory, and we have it really deep before making a trip out there. It reinforces the sense of personal identity, that's where the weak spot is."

"So that's what all this is for," said the girl suddenly. "Bless Our Home, Bless Our Identity Insurance."

"That's very perceptive of you, Miss Helena," said the Warden, and smiled. "Other Wardens have something like this. Tastes differ, of course, but I like this period—I took a major in Late Middle English. When you live on the edge of it, when you look out at it, when you go out into it, you need something. You need something solid, familiar—kind. You need identity insurance."

"I do," she said, "yes, I do. But I need that other thing too. You know."

"I see things for myself," said Kraag. "When can we start? I can't spare more than thirty standard hours."

"We can take the conditioning tomorrow morning, make the flip and be back within six hours."

"Good," said Kraag.

"Little Billy doesn't like it," said Merganser moodily.

"Then stay here. I'm sure the Warden can manage

11

without you," said Kraag with a touch of contempt for his heir-executive.

"No, I'll go. I'm not afraid of space-spooks. I believe in me, but not much else."

Paradine looked up at the grandfather clock as it softly intoned the Merton chime and struck five.

"We can talk about it later. Might I respectfully suggest a rest before dinner?"

They were still talking about it at dinner, at the end of a splendid *boeuf en daube* accompanied by a modest but satisfactory synthetic *Médoc*. Bill Merganser's hand slipped as he lowered his glass to the table, and the spilt wine soaked into the cloth like blood on a shirt-front.

"I'm a ranking player in fifteen different sports," he said, "I've even been on reserve for the marine decathlon—d'you know that?—but in maths I'm just a Charlie whosit. So tell me again, brother maestro, all in little words. They call this the End of the Universe. So why isn't it?"

"But it is," said Paradine. "The Universe ends here. It's the end of space. What lies beyond it is unspace, untime, unlaw, unpossibility."

"It sounds like falling through the hole in a zero," said Merganser, reaching for the bottle. "It still doesn't make sense."

"No one's ever claimed that it does. There's Hayakawa's equations, of course, they don't explain the phenomena, but they relate them to our universe. But they don't make sense either. The assymetries are impossible, frightening even. They say the old man went crazy trying to prove them."

"I met Hayakawa once," said Kraag unexpectedly. "A strange man. They say he was crazy even before he discovered the equations."

"H'excuse me, sir," said the old butler, "but would you wish me to serve the *crêpes suzette*, sir?"

The guests watched as the old man brought up the trolley and began the final stages of the ritual. Merganser, who had been slumped in his chair, watched

12

intently. As the critical moment came for the lighting of the brandy, he suddenly yelled: "Thunderfire!"

The old butler's hands jerked, the bottle toppled, and a sheet of flame flashed up with a blue glare. There was a smell of singed nylon and burnt brandy; as the smoke cleared, the old man's head appeared totally stripped of hair; the wrinkled naked plastiflesh looked singularly unconvincing. He addressed himself to Merganser:

"You cruddy-faced wall-eyed splay-eared slab-sided slobbery-nosed spavined left-footed heavy-arsed cack-handed undomesticated soddery snot-gobbling trumpery hermaphroditical constipated codswalloping decobblerized uneducated poxy parasitical son of an old git," he said rapidly.

"Smithers," said the Warden in a sharp tone of command, "you're forgetting yourself. I think you'd better go and lie down, and ask Mrs. Wiggins to serve the coffee."

The old butler stood rigid for a moment, and the faint clicking of relays could be heard, before he turned and doddered jerkily towards the door.

"Yes yes sir sir," he muttered in hollow tones, "I'm I'm very very sorry sorry I'm I'm sure sure sir sir."

"Thunderfire!" repeated Merganser in a loud voice, and sat back giggling. The robot jerked into a run, collided heavily with the doorpost and staggered off down the passage.

"That's the one trouble with these K59 models," said Paradine, "they're liable to break down unexpectedly under stress."

"I must remember that," said Kraag, "though I suppose it can happen to people too." He looked sourly across at Merganser, who seemed to have fallen asleep.

"Is that why they can't go out there," said Helena, "instead of you?"

"Quite right, Miss Helena. The human mind is still the most shockproof system of instrumentation in the universe."

"But why go at all?" she said. "If it's just there, and

13

nothing can help it—is it just one of those insane beautiful things that men do?"

"There's a reason," said Paradine. "It's the instability. Hayakawa's equations predicted that—and that's one reason we accept them. Normally the Limits are expanding, and the Nothing is going back. But every so often it breaks in, hugely."

Kraag nodded. "In 2758," he said, "the breakthrough in Tau Seventeen. It took out three whole galaxies. Just think, three galaxies, millions of stars, millions of planets."

"Oh that," said Helena, "it was on video, you know. The Last Days of New Pompeii, they had real orgies in that one, it was utterly magnetic, and the sun exploded."

"It wasn't like that," said Paradine patiently. "The Limits shifted, the frame of reference changed, and three galaxies just stopped being probable. Of course, the thing stabilised after a while. And what they don't tell you on video is that the salvage-sweepers went through afterwards and found the debris—queer things."

"What things?"

"Planets made of rust. Thousands of two-headed lions. Carnivorous stones. Izaak Newton in a paper coffin. Radioactive lead. Suns that absorbed heat. A little man ten millimetres tall made of collapsium. In the end they just set up warning beacons and left it."

"How utterly baroque," she said with a shiver.

"That's when they created the Wardens' Corps. Whenever there's a galaxy near the Limits, the Corps puts out a planetoid, sets up a post on it—and here we are."

"It costs a crillion dollars to put you here," said Kraag, "one man and a neurotic robot against all that Nothing." He spread out his huge, meaty hands. "What could you do?"

"We go into it and observe," said Paradine matter-of-factly. "We think we know some of the signs of instability."

"But what could you do?" insisted Kraag. "If it happened?"

14

"Switch on an all-band screamer, and run like hell," said Paradine.

There was a gentle tap on the door, and a motherly-looking person entered and began to serve the coffee. The robot's bald plastiflesh head had been replaced by pink cheeks, steel-rimmed glasses and grey corkscrew curls with a mob-cap, the ancient dinner-jacket by an ample-bosomed grey dress and immaculate white apron.

"I do hope," she said, "as how you'll find it in your heart to excuge pore Smithers, sir, what is quite overcome with shame for his stravagant behaviour. In a proper taking he is, the pore soul, and I left him a-sitting in the kitchen and Cook a-comforting him with a little drop of salvolatile, and something hot to follow."

Paradine passed the brandy decanter and Merganser filled his balloon-glass generously.

"Not that you can really blame him for being occagionally indispoged, sir, if you will allow me to say so, for he's been in service now man and boy for sixty year come Michaelmas—"

"Mrs. Wiggins—"

"—what with his arthuritis and the way the young servants are nowadays and the tradesmen giving no service whatsocomever not like they was accustomed to—"

"If it needs rehuxleyizing, send the account to Billy," muttered Kraag.

"—but as I always says to him, I says, compoge yourself Mr. Smithers, I says, for things must get worse nor they get better, I says, and every cloud has a silver lining, I says—"

"Please Mrs. Wiggins—"

"—and it's always darkest before the dawn, I says, and there's worse things happen at sea, I says, and—"

"Thunderfire!" yelled Merganser, lurching to his feet. Mrs. Wiggins flung her apron over her face and rushed from the room in screaming hysterics.

Merganser beamed down at them with a drunken smile on his beautiful albino face, and the words of a

15

great revelation trembling on his lips. He loved them all.

"Love," he said. "Nothing. I love nothing." He shook his head wisely. "There are limits, even to nothing." He lifted his brandy-balloon to them. "Here's to you, dolly, and your big blue eyes and your little hard heart. And here's to you, Boss Kraag, and your galactic charge-account. And here's to you, Warden, you dutiful bastard." He drained the glass and sent it smashing into the hearth. The effort spun him around and he fell headlong on to the hearthrug, where he fell fast asleep. The robot-hound sniffed at him and raised its head in a melancholy howl.

After Merganser had been carried up to bed, the others retired to their rooms, where the rough sheets were faintly perfumed with synthetic lavender. Helena Kraag tossed restlessly in bed, her mind full of jumbled memories and bad dreams. Even when a relay clicked and turned on the soothing noise of rain on the roof, it only disturbed her with shifting recollections of the long surf on New Bondi, and the sifting snowfalls on the winter planet of Tolstoi, and the lost Rain Gardens of Greater Avalon.

At last she got up, zipped on a quilted coverall, and wandered along the corridor and down into the hall. Lights came on as she passed, and as she opened the door into the parlour, the log fire began to blaze, the grandfather-clock began its tick-tock, and the robot-hound thumped his tail on the hearthrug in welcome. With a vague idea that people once used to read themselves to sleep, she went across to the bookshelf and puzzled over the books with the leather bindings and queer old titles in gold lettering: The Compleat Angler ... Boswell's Life of Johnson ... Treasure Island ... The Once and Future King ... Holmes's Practical Handbook of Bee-Culture.

Something about this one interested her, and she reached out for it. But it would not leave the shelf; instead, the whole bookcase sank back and slid to one side, revealing a long corridor which was quite unlike the rest of the house. It had curved metal walls and a

16

series of side-doors; but she walked slowly past these, and stopped only at the end, where the door carried, in large red fluorescent letters, the notice:

OBSERVATORY
NO ADMISSION BEYOND
THIS POINT FOR
UNCONDITIONED PERSONNEL

She ignored this, and palmed the release-plate; the door slid open.

The room was a dome, about fifty metres high; from the faint vibration of machinery beneath her feet, she guessed that it was the upper half of a single metal sphere. She walked between ranks of controls and monitors, and stopped for a moment at one labelled HEISENBERG SYSTEM NO. I, a tall console of indicator lights, all at green.

Then came the scopes and scanners, and the monitor screens with shifting meaningless patterns—the endless undulating graphs, the radars charting impossible cloud-continents, the dark field sprinkled with random scintillations. In the half-light under the tall dome, she stared at the jewel-lights, the ghost-shapes, the luminous mathematical abstracts, and listened to their soft voices which sang and twittered and ululated at her. One of them could even count numbers, if you stood close enough to it: 343, 454, 707, 717, 464, 222 ... keeping time to an endless triple pattern of coloured dots which danced on a dark screen.

"Magnetic," she murmured to them, "magnetic but baroque. You know."

She could have stayed there forever, in that singing place. She would have liked to sleep there, if there had been anywhere to lie down; but there was nothing except a swivel-seat at the far end of the dome in front of a large circular recess in the wall, so she sat there. Bright red letters began flashing on the console in front of her:

URGENT URGENT
INTERDICTED TO ALL
UNCONDITIONED PERSONNEL

She ignored that and pressed the black button to her right, but nothing happened. Then she flipped the red switch marked Override, on her left. There was a humming sound. The circular recess opened like an iris, and she peered out through the transparency beyond.

At first, it seemed just darkness, a night without stars; but as her eyes adjusted, she began to see a vast vagueness which corresponded in some way to all that the machines were graphing and scintillating and cooing and chirruping behind her. It was neither light nor dark, neither matter nor space, neither form nor formlessness. It had no dimension, but it had, in a way, magnitude; it did not seem to move, yet was filled with a ceaseless purposeless immeasurable activity. It burned; it extended; it loomed; it sundered; it drenched; it tore; it sagged; it energized; it bled; it strummed; it deliquesced; it formicated; it torqued; it transposed. Its name was legion; it was all and any, but it was also one.

It was when she perceived the unity that the room began to tilt, and all that enormity was not in front of her, but below her. Behind (above) her the machines began to scream and rasp, and the number-machine said; zero zero zero, zero zero zero ... Without movement, she was falling and a scream rose in her throat and would not stop. She was still screaming when her father and Paradine, roused by the alarm-klaxon, came running, and Paradine touched the switch which closed that dreadful eye, and the machines went back to their fluting and whispering.

The robot came gliding swiftly along the corridor, wearing a white coat and still adjusting its pale freckled Scottish-medico face and russet wig.

"She's in shock, Doctor McGillicuddy," murmured Paradine. "Used the Eye without preconditioning."

Helena had stopped screaming when the Eye closed, but she sat rigidly catatonic, hands gripped to the arms of the chair, staring in front of her with mad blue eyes. The doctor reached out; she felt the cold touch of a subcutaneous spray in her arm, and slumped forward on to the console.

18

"Och the puir wee wilfu' lassie," said Doctor McGillicuddy in fatherly tones. "Has she been keekin' thru' the Ee the noo? Eh, but yon's a daft thing tae do, ye ken. But we'll soon hae ye to richts, ma puir wee sleekit timorous cowerin' beastie. Aye, we'll gie ye a wee bit condeetioning, foreby, juist tae restorre y'r sense o' pairrsonal identity, ye ken."

She was eased gently on to a trolley and wheeled away between the ranks of glowing machines which crooned lullabies to her, and the doctor said roguishly: "Ah wumman in our hours o' ease, rreluctant coy and hairrd tae please, when pain and sorro' rring the broo—but ah'm the wee meenistering angel the noo."

He wheeled the trolley into the corridor and through the nearest of the side doors. This room was also domed, but much smaller, and lit by a warm rosy light which centered on a globe hung from the ceiling. As she lay there alone, the light drew her towards it, and a voice which sounded like her own began to chant softly:

> "I! I am I—I
> am me—Me is
> I—I see me, I
> see you! I am
> not you—You are
> not me—You is
> not me. You and I
> are we—We are
> not they! They are
> not me. They see
> me—I see them!
> What are they? Who
> am I? Who sees I?
> I am I see
> you are not they
> see I am who?
> . . . .

And she dreamed that she met a girl named Helena Kraag and they walked hand in hand through the forest where the jewelled birds twittered from the metal trees.

19

TWO

THE THREE MEN shared an early breakfast. It was a silent meal. Bill Merganser, pale and a little shaky, could only murmur: "Brother, that's quite a synthesiser you've got," and sip his fortified fruit-juice. Kraag scanned through a spool of the galactic share-index, which had just come off the ship's communicator. Paradine, who had run through a hypno-paedic course on the big ship's instrumentation while he slept, was mentally checking out on emergency drills. Neither old Smithers nor Mrs. Wiggins was in attendance. At a nod from Kraag, Paradine led the way down the hidden corridor to the conditioning room.

When they returned, Helena was wandering up and down the room, nibbling from the array of hot dishes on the sideboard. They trooped out into the garden, where the artificial sky was flecked with small convincing white clouds; bees and doves had been replaced by the trilling of a skylark.

A tall rangy figure dressed in faded bush-shirt and slacks lounged against the sundial and rolled a cigarette.

"How does it manage the height?" muttered Merganser.

"Telescopic legs," said Paradine. "Self-compensating. And arms. Meet Ron," he added in a louder voice. "He's a bush-pilot—comes over when we need a bit of help. Ron, we're going to take a quick trip otherside."

"G'day," said Ron, his brown leathery face crumpling into a smile as he shook hands all round. "You folks comin' fer a flip? It's a grayday fer it—one outer the box."

Paradine nodded towards the tall lopsided shape of the Kraag ship on the other side of the hedge. "We're going in that one," he said.

"Cripes, yer won't get me in that bus, sport, not fer

a walkabout in the never-never. They don't make Heisenbergs that bluddy big. Yer wouldn't stand Buckley's chance."

"It's got two of everything," said Paradine. "It's as safe as—as Sydney Harbour Bridge."

"Ah, goodole Sinney, wish I wuz there now." The robot fell obediently into step beside him. "I mus' be or'f me bluddy rocker to go otherside in a big bluddy can like that jus' fer this crowder bluddy drongoes."

They entered the ship and the airlocks hissed shut behind them. Paradine eased himself into the control-chair and began checking the main board. Seated beside him, Ron unscrewed the covering of his upper left index finger, disclosing a metal jack which he inserted into a socket in the autopilot. The robot became rigid, but the ship's intercom began to address them with a faint trace of Old Orstrilian accent:

"Ship secured and ready for lift off. All systems go. Auxiliary drive activated. Ship's gravity takes over—now. Standing by for instructions."

The drone of the motors steadied, and there was a faint jar as the ship's own gravity-field took over. Paradine slipped the flight-tapes into the slot in the autopilot, and looked towards Kraag. The big man nodded, and Paradine pulled down the operating handle.

"Ship lifting in five seconds from—now. Five four three two one lift-off."

The drives droned down the scale into silence. Paradine waited until the main drive cut in before he left his place to join the others, who were sitting in the loungers at the other end of the control-deck, watching the retro-screen. A small service-robot was handing round coffee with its delicate metal claws; Merganser sent it off for a scotch.

"Take a good look," said Paradine, "that's the universe that man's always known. Nice empty space, nice friendly stars, all shipshape and Einstein's equations. Soon we shan't be seeing it for a few hours: believe me, you'll be glad to see it come back."

On the dark screen, a hazy spiral showed in the

lower left corner; the rest was thinly scattered with pinpoints of dull reddish light.

"But there are so few," said Helena. "Where have they all gone?"

"Don't forget the velocity of recession is fantastic out here. We're moving away too fast to see many of them."

"Remember the rhyme, dolly," said Merganser, downing his drink, and went on in a little-boy voice:

"Doppler, Doppler, overhead,
Receding stars shift down to red,
As the speed approaches C
Stars no longer shine on me."

Paradine pointed to the spiral: "That's G 431, M'Boto's Galaxy," he said. "That's why I'm here. It's pretty thinly settled, as yet, and there's nothing much else around."

"But there are people there, you know, people," said the girl, "all this way. People grow on everything, like mould. They're everywhere."

"It was bound to happen," said Kraag, "as soon as the earthside population began to double every generation. They found anti-grav and the overdrive just in time. Now nothing can stop us. And why not? People are wealth. The whole of Old Earth wasn't worth more than about eighty five crillion solars. Now look at us."

"Mould," said Helena, "blight, vermin, fungus. We're eating the universe alive. Nothing but stinking people everywhere. What happens when we run out of universe?"

"Perhaps by then we'll have found out what's really happening on the otherside," said Paradine. "Perhaps men could live, even in that. They can live in almost anything else, with the right equipment."

"Yes, they do, you know," said Helena. "On icecaps and at the bottom of oceans. On desert worlds and asteroids. It's that sad old urge to multiply. Wherever there's a bit of rock or mud below boiling point, you'll find men beginning to crawl over it." She turned to her father. "Boss Kraag, why don't you buy me a planet—a big beautiful planet, and I could live on it all alone with a few robots, and have friends when I wanted, and be quite alone when I wanted?"

"It's the one paragraph in the intergalactic convention that can neither be bent nor broken," grumbled Kraag. "No exclusive property in any planetary body."

Merganser finished his third large scotch, loosened his hand-embroidered collar, and settled back in the lounger. "What's wrong with people?" he said. "I like people. I hate solitude—it's simply mordant, you see, fugue, derelict. I love to feel a crowd around me, like nice animals, all breathing together."

"All drinking together, your crowd," said the girl without looking at him. "If you like people so much, why do you use that stuff to get away from them?"

"Look, dolly, that's the—that's the real example. See it, the drink gives me a sense of the oneness, the all."

"The oneness the all," she mimicked. "A lot of sad little people, all stewed together in their own fat, all cheap and sloshy." She leaned towards him, her eyes crazy with contempt. Merganser dropped his glass and spat.

"You gaudy unnatural man-hating—"

Kraag's enormous left hand clamped about his face and sent him sprawling across the cabin.

"Listen to me, Billy boy, and you, Helena. You're my heir-executive, and you're going to marry my daughter. It suits me to have it that way. But I warn you, Billy boy, I warn you. I made you out of nothing to be my heir and my daughter's husband. I gave you whatever you've got, and I can take it away again— all of it—credits, exclusive sports-clubs, dollies, space-runabouts—the boxful. Even your hand-embroidered clothes. Even your face."

Merganser, on all fours on the floor, began to weep, and his nose was bleeding.

"I could make a dozen more to take your place, any day, out of nothing. And you, Warden Paradine, will forget what has been said and done here."

23

"At your orders, Boss Kraag," said Paradine stiffly. "With your permission, I'll see heir-executive Merganser to his cabin. We'll be making entry in about ten minutes."

When he returned to the cabin, Helena was staring at the retro-screen, and bald-headed Kraag loomed huge behind her. M'Boto's Galaxy had faded to a dim red dot; there was nothing else on the screen but darkness. Then it flickered out. The intercom said:

"Ship now entering nonspace. All Heisenbergs go. All external phenomena random; no indication of purposive trends."

Helena noticed that a row of monitor screens above the auxiliary board, which had been blank throughout the journey, had now come to life. The instruments she had seen last night were there in miniature like a child's playthings—luminous graphs, tiny menacing radar-shapes, scintillations, coloured dots dancing no bigger then pinheads, while a little voice whispered: 707, 292, 808, 565 . . .

Kraag gestured impatiently. "Why can't we get direct observation?" he said.

"Strict instructions, Boss Kraag," said Paradine. "That's why I sealed your viewports. Anything you saw probably wouldn't mean anything; it would be worse if it did, though. You can have a good look through the Eye when we return."

Kraag grunted. "It's a long way to come just for instrument readings," he said. "I did this for you, Helena. Why did you want to come?"

"It was something new," said Helena indifferently. "I thought it would be otherwise, you know, lonesome."

"There's something coming up," said Paradine, and pointed. Some of the scintillations remained fixed, like minute stars; the cloud-pattern dissolved into shimmering lines; one of the graphs assumed the regular form of a sine-wave, shivered and all dissolved.

"What was it said?" Kraag said.

"Just a local random probability. They form and

24

dissolve quite frequently. Maybe that's all we'll see. It's often like that on a routine trip."

"But what does it mean?" said Helena crossly.

"Something might be going to happen. A star, a man, a photon, something we've never heard of. It might be a whole world, living on its own terms."

They stared in silence for a time, while tentative patterns formed and dissolved, often the merest flicker on the screens. The tiny stars held, the cloud contracted to a point, and the coloured dots danced into a figure-of-eight. The voice whispered: 245, 246, 247, 357, 358, 359, 210 . . . Paradine leaned closer, and said: "That's interesting, I've only seen it once before. It's a stasis of some kind, perhaps a dimensional inversion."

"That's mordant," said Helena.

"We can only guess," said Paradine. "Is it your wish to have lunch now, Boss Kraag?" Kraag grunted, and Paradine gave orders to the service-robot.

"Just on three sidereal hours," said Paradine. "We'll be turning any minute now."

"I still don't know how you navigate in this muck," said Kraag.

"Basically it's inertial, but the trick is, we have to create our own field as we go along. It does something to the unspace, you know. We're carrying around a set of our own physical laws where there aren't supposed to be any. It seems to upset it, you might think."

"Makes the natives hostile," chuckled Kraag suddenly. "Who wouldn't? It wouldn't be sanitary to stay around here too long."

"That's why we keep moving—"

"Your attention please," broke in the intercom voice. "Ship approaching turnaround. Commencing return—now."

Kraag leaned forward for a closer look at one of the scanners.

"Grief of nothings," he said, "there's a ship out there. Are you double-beaming us, Warden?"

"A ghost-ship," said Paradine, "look closer." He

25

touched the switch which zoomed the scan into large focus.

"It's a mark ten runabout," said Kraag flatly.

"It's us," said Paradine.

"Mirror-image? Mirage? Mimicry?"

"Not quite. It's out there, and it looks like us, is all. They sometimes appear about turnaround."

"I'm glad I can't see inside it," muttered Helena.

"It's a thing Hayakawa talked about," said Paradine. "A—what?—crystallization, polarization, something like, if something from our universe intruded into this. As I said, we upset it, and this is one way it reacts."

"Perhaps it envies us," said the girl. The image fragmented and began to dissolve.

They continued to watch the screens as they ate.

"Do patrols always come back?" said Helena with a sudden shiver.

"Once in a while—a long while—they don't. But you're quite safe, Miss Helena, we're turning back now and it's been pure routine all the way."

"*How* many don't make it?" said Kraag sharply.

"Maybe—one in fifty. But the average improves all the time."

"Damn the average in a place where there aren't any averages."

The pattern changed again. Stars blinked, dots melted into coloured rain, a graph undulated, the cloud turned into a rippling circle.

"Now what?" said Kraag.

"Some kind of temporal. Probably a simple time-pulse—forward-back, forward-back. That would be a swampy one to get caught in. But see, we're through."

Quite suddenly, the screen flared and went out. All the jewelled indicators flashed red, and an alarm klaxon roared. The robot-pilot slumped suddenly in his chair. The lights flickered madly.

"It's all right," said Paradine jumping up, "the fail-safe auxiliaries . . ."

The klaxon cut off, the lights steadied, the indicators went red-green-red, and all went out again. Ron the robot jerked into life and collapsed. Even the

26

klaxon cut off. In the total darkness, Paradine's voice sounded flat and unbelieving. "The auxiliaries—they've gone too. I'll do what I can."

He fumbled for a light, but before he could find it, the door to the cabins slid open and Bill Merganser stood there with a glow-lamp. The whole of the control-deck seemed filled with its cold green light.

"Just one thing your tame geniuses didn't extrapolate, Boss Kraag," said the young man with a malicious grin. "The main control-ducts run through the wall of my cabin. I knew that. I just had to lift a couple of panels—" He held up a portable cutter in his gloved hand.

"Now I'll kill you, Billy boy," rumbled Kraag softly.

"I'm in command of this ship," said Paradine in his command voice. "Boss Kraag, I hold you responsible for this man's custody. Wait here and don't get in my way." As he spoke, he was opening a locker and taking out a glow-light, a portable tool-kit and some spare leads; then he made for Merganser's cabin at a dead run.

The open wall-panels and the severed cables were plain to see. Swiftly he sorted out the ends and clamped on the spare leads, first to one system, then to the other. As he did so, the cabin lights came on and the air-intakes began to hiss faintly. He leaned his forehead and his damp palms against the cool metal bulkhead, and he could feel the vibration of the drives as they picked up again.

When the lights flashed up on the control-deck, Kraag pushed Merganser contemptuously into one of the loungers. "The rebellion's over, Billy boy," he said. "And when we get back I'm going to put you right back where you came from. Thank you, Warden."

But Paradine was standing motionless in the doorway, staring at the auxiliary board where, among the indicator all at green, one row blinked out a sinister red.

"It's the Heisenberg shields," he said. "They're dead. I must check."

Fifteen minutes later when he returned to the control-deck, the others had not changed position—

Merganser slumped in the lounger, Kraag standing over him with his huge meaty hands dangling at his sides, Helena staring at the screens which had resumed their random patterns. Ron the robot was again sitting rigidly erect.

"They're gone," said Paradine quietly. "The main generators are fused, and I think part of the outside gear has carried away."

"Warden," said Kraag, "you get us out of this and I'll give you the wealth of a whole planet—a rich planet."

"I'll do what I can, Boss Kraag. But please try to understand this. We've lost our only protection against all that out there. Not only that, we've lost the operational field by which the ship guided itself. I'll try; I hope the course holds good. It's like trying to run a ship planetside without a gyrocompass, without even dead reckoning. But we might come out—somewhere."

"And when we do, I'm going to rub you out bit by bit, my heir-executive Hyperion Merganser."

"Hyperion—phthack," said Merganser. "That's the name you gave me with the plastic-surgery. You know what they really called me when I was a kid? Hippo, you know, after some mythical dinosaur, all blubberfat and big teeth." He giggled. "That was me, a dirty fat tough slobbo. It's still me, Boss Kraag, and all your high-class robot plastisurgeons couldn't change it."

He settled back in the lounger, while the other watched the screens and listened. The time had come for confidences: there was no point in quarrelling.

"I grew up that way, in a place called Rackstraw's Planet. It ought to be rich, it grows food for New Pittsburgh, the mining planet next door. But all the wealth sticks in the gullets of Boss Rackstraw and his entrepreneurs, and most of the food is grown by poor little peon-farmers. I had no parents. I lived with an old woman I called Granny: she bought me from the orphanage. She had a little rundown place on the edge of the badlands, growing potatonuts and mutated cabbage. A creek ran through it, but it ran almost dry in summer, and she couldn't afford to build the smallest dam, and most of the little credit we made went on buying tank-water. Oh my grief, it was poor. And we lived mostly on our own crops— potatonut bread and cabbage soup—phthack."

He took a neat scotch from the service robot and gagged on it as he swallowed.

"I worked, oh I worked. She, the old woman, used to sit in the shanty all day, drinking the stuff they call wormwood wine—that's where the rest of the credits went. But she always knew when I stopped work, you know, and she'd come out with this strip of plastoline and beat me bug-eyed. She had a tongue too; she could curse like Viridianese swedge-driver. I was blubbery, but I was hard.

"But there was one thing, know this, there was this creek I told you. In summer it was cracked mud, but in spring and autumn the cool freshes came down, roiling, and it filled from bank to bank, but shallow, and it had flat yellow fish in it that were poison to eat. And I'd jump in, rags and all, and wash the stink out of myself, and chase the yellow fish, and come out red with the mud in the water. And grief of birds, she'd wipe me down with that strip of plastoline till I fell on the ground, and she got tired of it. But I'd go back again, it was so good. So one day I couldn't stand it any more, and I was big then, so I pushed the old woman in the creek, and she washed away." He giggled into his glass. "I still dream of her flopping about, she was drunk, and her dirty grey hair streaming out in the muddy water. Then they sent me back to the orphanage, and I ran away and hung around the only city on Rackstraw's Planet. I starved and served a length in gaol, but the beatings were no worse than Granny's. Then I met you, Boss Kraag."

"A dirty overgrown slummer, trying to finesse my baggage outside the spaceport," said Kraag. "If I'd turned you over, they'd had your right hand off for that."

"Thanks for zero," said Merganser, "I went to work for you instead. Oh you hadn't the smell of money on you then, Boss Kraag; the cases I tried to finesse were

29

real dunnage. You were just starting, and you wanted a local man for a little job. You tell it, Boss."

"It was pure and simple," said Kraag, smiling as he remembered. "Those were good days, think, when I began to see the way up. That old fool Rackstraw and his clan never realised that they held New Pittsburgh in a vice. They squeezed their croppers for pfennings; they should have been squeezing the metal barons for their blood. Control Rackstraw's Planet, you control New Pittsburgh. I saw this slummer—yes, this one—he was tough and brainy then. So I bought him cheap and set him to build me a local combination."

"What bodies, what minds," said Merganser. "Muck-sledders, lefties, gone-overs, crawlers, ester-happies, dafties also, all savage and with nothing to lose. And outlaws in the badlands—that's where we flew in the equipment. It was junk, but it worked soso. And one day we hit the Rackstraws when they were having a big clanfest at their summer camp—wiped them away, littlies, the boxful."

He took another glass from the service-robot, and Kraag did the same.

"Then I flew in my management," said Kraag, "and told New Pittsburgh what we wanted, and cut off the food. When they scratched up a fleet of freighters to drop on us, I told them we'd spray the whole planet and sterilize it. It was no ploy—I had the stuff all loaded and ready. I would have done it. So presently I had New Pittsburgh, as much as I needed, and first thing I switched Rackstraw's Planet over to mechanical harvesting, so that no one could put that ploy on me."

"What about the people?" said Helena in a low voice.

"What would you guess? I didn't want people there."

"Those were fine times," said Merganser. "I loved you then, Boss Kraag."

They touched glasses in the old ritual, and drank.

"I built my first war fleet out of New Pittsburgh metals," said Kraag. "A lot of worlds were new then and getting rich and frightened. I found a fat one,

Calydon, getting a little soft, with hardy neighbours. Sold them a packaged scale five warfleet, complete from one H-bomb right down to two thousand stunguns and five hundred units of bottled plasma. They used it for a sanitary exercise on their near neighbours. Wiped the system clean, kept Calydon safe and fat and happy. That upset two neighbouring systems. One of them, the Mandala worlds, I sold a scale three package—they were big, a confederacy. They wiped Calydon. The others—oh, now, Samurai—one planet, but populous and hardy—bought a scale five, but when the Mandalans attacked they made such a dent that the confederacy hauled off and signed a treaty. After that it was like wholesale groceries—how many worlds, Billy boy?"

"Fifty, sixty," said Merganser. "Ruritan, New Taiwan, Lilliput, Nifelheim—"

"Merdeka, Full House, Kamikaze, Bread—" added Kraag.

"Cosa Nostra, Dunroamin, Double Oh Seven—"

"Poenamo, Bellissima, Lord Inigo's Folly—" Kraag began to laugh.

"Maryellen Murgatroyd—grief of suns, the dafty names—"

"Kelly's Eye, Nouvelle Provence, Santiago Major, Rutherford—"

"Cuchulain, Malebolge, Copperhead, Beulahland—"

"Elsinore, Hidalgo, Vermin, Thousand Flowers—"

Laughing, they touched glasses.

"If there wasn't trouble," said Merganser, "I made it. I got to be good at the thing—persuader, fixer, frightener, whatever was needful. I was big and ugly, and I built you a big ugly organisation, Boss. But things began to plane out, go smooth, and we went smooth too. That's when you bought me all the high-class surgery, and I went in looking like a pig, and came out looking like a video-star."

"It was the best," said Kraag, "and the old colleges too, the athletics scholarships, the good clubs. I bought you all that, and inside, I knew, you still looked like a pig."

"Then why did you set him up to marry me?" cried Helena, her face white.

"You guessed, you know," jeered Merganser.

"Ninety minutes since turnaround," said Paradine. "We're half-way back, with luck." His voice remained level; he did not mention that the monitorscreens were giving incoherent readings, and that red lights were beginning to wink on and off among the green indicators. There was a silence, then Kraag said:

"I say now that your best was good, Billy boy. You moved along with it all the way, the boardrooms, the spacejumpers, the tall hotels. Then we didn't have to be simple any more, but had associates and combines, and went for the entrepots and the power-nuclei. How many worlds was it? I don't need the details any-more."

"Two thousand, think, spread over the right places in three galaxies. Rich, oh rich."

Kraag's glass bounced and rang on the floor, and his huge hands tightened on the arms of the lounger. "And now I've got to sit in my crillion solar ship and wait for that muck out there to take me."

"We'll get through, Boss Kraag, we'll get through," said Paradine. But he watched the winking red lights slowly marching across the board, as in some game of supercheckers, and the whispering voice was saying: 2709, 1, 452, 453, 454, 66, 2709 . . . Helena could hear it too; she looked across at him, and then turned to Kraag.

"When did you decide that he was to marry me?"

"You know that," said Merganser with a sour grin. "It was when your mother ran off with Sobieski."

"I had the most beautiful woman in two hundred worlds," said Kraag, "and she left me to run off with a cheap lawyer."

"Where are they now?"

Kraag hunched his huge shoulders: there was sweat on his bald head.

"Would I know? Space is big, and they had money."

"I know," said Helena suddenly, "I found her. And you know too, Boss Kraag. On Venusberg, you know,

I traced her there. I thought at least she'd be up at the top of the Hill, maybe even with some sweet little desk job. But she wasn't there, not in the big houses, where they have the soft music and the balconies looking down on the sea. Not half-way down, where they have the masquerades and the funny mirrors. But right down, in the dirtiest room in the worst house at the bottom of the hill. When I found her, she didn't even know me."

Kraag watched her, sweating. The army of red lights now dominated the indicator-board.

"I got her out. I sent her to that place with the insane name—oh, Hemlock, yes—where people go when they want to die soon and happy. It cost much money," she added with childish malice, "your money."

"If it makes you happy, sweetheart—" muttered Kraag, but she ignored him.

"That's when I started to have bad dreams, and you sent me to such beautiful doctors, all that money could buy, but the dreams won't go away."

One by one the green lights went out; they could feel the ship weaving and labouring as the autopilot struggled desperately for control.

"Well Warden, virtuous Limitary Warden Paradine," said Merganser, "this is the night of truth. What's your story? The good little boy who never turned aside, never looked back?"

"Not quite," said Paradine, deliberately turning his dark eyes from the monitors, and he smiled. "Not at all, in fact. I grew up on Thorshammer—it was a mining planet like your New Pittsburgh, rather. You know I never saw the sky till I was twenty? Nothing but a grey smokecap, and there was grit everywhere and oily film. At least it was where I lived—streets of tall old concrete-slab buildings, run up in a hurry, patched and cobbled, never renewed."

Glancing at the board, he saw that the green lights were few, and he felt strangely at ease.

"I don't know who my parents were, and I was never lucky enough to get into an orphanage. They didn't have them on Thorshammer. Littlies like us,

33

we scavenged, there was plenty of refuse about. But it was cold, grief it was cold there, and we used to creep up to the exhaust ducts from the factory air-conditioners, and sleep in the hot stale air. There were gangs, you know, the customary thing in a place like that. And rough too. But I got to be number two man in the Death's Head Hussars—they had dafty names like that. Then I met the holy man."

"I'd guess it," jeered Merganser, "a holy man, a christbearer, think?"

Paradine nodded. "A christbearer. You meet them sometimes, and mostly in places like that. A little man, grey, hardy, he worked as sweeper in one of the plants. He lived on nothing, he gave away every centavo, and he slept in a hole in one of the tenements where they'd ripped out a boiler and forgot to put in a new one. That was how I met him."

He suddenly knew two things, that the last green light was on the blink and that the girl was looking at him with sane eyes, and he felt a sudden shock of loss.

"One night there was a big scramble in our precinct," he said to her, "six gangs altogether, and we were on the losers. I am hurt and I am running, I don't know where, and there are ten, twelve shivmen after me, hollering and laughing. Then an iron service-door opens in the wall, and someone pulls me in, and that's all, for a time."

He sighed. It was nearly over.

"When I woke up it was in the hole in the basement where this old man lived, this padre Martin. I was lying on a pile of packing-paper, it was his own bed. I stayed there a while and he looked after me—I was cut quite a bit, think, and he knew the old medicine, and he fed me on good broth. When I was fit again, I'd go out into the streets, but I'd go back often at nights. We talked for hours, and he taught me to read—yes, read out of old paper books. We read stories, all kinds, the old ones about Adam and Ulysses and Christ and Arthur, all strange to me then. I'd tell you more, but we haven't time . . .

"Well, you know, one night there was another

34

scramble, and the stormtroopers were doing a razzia, and I was pulled in. They knew something about old Martin—the Party was in power then, and the christbearers were something they didn't like. So I told about him. It took so little to make me tell, just hot food and a clean bed. He passed me in a corridor as they brought him in you know, he smiled at me, and made that secret sign they have—" Paradine sketched a tiny x in the air with the tip of his index finger.

"What happened to him?" asked Helena.

"Re-educated," said Paradine, "that meant the deep mines ... After that the Party looked after me, and put me through school and college. I could have gone all the way with them. But when I heard about the Wardens, I applied, and even the Party couldn't stop the Limitary Authority, and I'm here."

"Brother," said Merganser, and reaching forward put his right hand over Paradine's. "We did our work and took our wages; but you knew it."

In the silence, they felt that the vibration of the drives had stopped; the ship was adrift.

"We aren't going to get through," said Kraag.

"No," said Paradine, rising to his feet.

Merganser began to laugh uncontrollably. "You—Boss Kraag—Miss Helena—Warden—me—did we know —what we were looking for? Perhaps it's here—in the nothing."

"Look," said Helena, "oh what does it mean?" She pointed to the monitor-screens where the patterns had now frozen, but flickered slowly on and off.

"Stasis," said Paradine, "dimensional inversion, total instability."

"That's buggered it," said the voice of the ship's intercom. The robot jerked to its feet and began walking towards the far wall of the control-deck, stripping off its mask and cladding as it did so. The room was changing shape, belling outwards at the end, and the walls vibrated and stank and dissolved, opening out onto a vast floor of darkness. The robot ran free, stretching up as he ran, babbling in a last spasm of his tapes:

"Do not come down the ladder mister prichard i

have taken it away look you bach and when the old troubleandstrife told me i couldn't adamandeve it till i'd taken a ballofchalk up the applesandpears and seen it with me own mincepies for ah belong tae glasgow and a man's a man for a'that if you'll pardon the expression sir seeing as howcomewhatsoever five four three two one liftoff and who'll come a waltzing matilda with meeee . . ."

As it leapt and ran, its body stretched taller and taller, an attenuated metal spider kilometres high, until there was nothing left but the giant head which melted, raining tears of white-hot metal through the void. The ship tilted suddenly, and without a sound Boss Kraag and Billy boy, Miss Helena and the Warden spilled out. They fell for a symptotic time through infinite space towards the floor of darkness, which grew smaller, contracting to a point. When they met it, they

THREE

entered through zones and categories into the small time of nowhere until the season came when it (what?) began to snow green butterflies or something rather similar. There (where?) was a nucleus for ice world and in its time they sat for a space, unintegrated. Life itself, impossibly but not improbably, went on, nor did the rest seem important, since none of it was necessary. Before them an unpicturable landscape dissolved and redissolved, without sound, but they could taste it. It was musty.

Then (when?) a sound began, like a horse galloping across drums, and this was Bill Merganser's heart beating, which filled the world with solemn noise. He lay staring up at the vortices which formed and reformed above them. Kraag shivered with cold, his great teeth clenched; Helena huddled beside him in a delirium of euphoria, able to fly if she wished; Paradine sweated. If (when?) a thing could be recalled, it would be known, the heat made him think. And that was it (which?); *I*. A letter, word, image, a man standing in a place, but who? *I am I*. Comforting and rosy recollections of the conditioning-room broke through the sensory deformations.

"I am I," he said aloud, using his mouth with careful precision, like a remote-handling device.

"I am me," said the others, and they followed one another in the complex crosstalk of the conditioning chant.

Now they could at least assume contingencies, and the flux stiffened for sufficient time to appear tall (slow?), irregular (polytropic?), viable (relevant?).

Paradine moved stiffly to his feet, and called to the others, and several times later they were gathered and he thought humbly: "Climb." It was all, so that he led them stumbling across the reticulated cracks of

37

the ice-pavement. Words were nothing; it was a place of things.

After (in?) a time of sleep, they floundered across a river of wind and sat down together among the sounds of metal.

Riddled with fever, Kraag's voice jerked out: "What? is? this? place?"

"Randomness," muttered Paradine.

"I've heard," said Merganser. "Of such a planet."

"Insane," murmured Helena, "look. How depraved is all."

It seemed likely that they would climb the mountain, for it was now beside them. Paradine gathered them with the force of his eyes, and pointed to the crest, where a small rolling golden sun reclined upon the high plateau.

"Here," he said. "Now."

To them his hand seemed to touch the sun, but he did not burn; only for a microsecond he too was golden.

The way of the mountain was neither up nor down, neither long nor short, the journey either years or kilometres. They climbed and flew; they fell and swam; they walked and thought. A shaft of gravel or a fallen dolmen was overcome with arduous cunning; cliffs or cataracts passed by them as they slept or did not sleep. Always the mountain flowed and faded; only the golden sun, polarised to their intruding entities, lay placidly above those terraces which no astonishment could survey.

If it was air it blazed; if it was sound it froze. Swarms of boulders drifted by incuriously. If it was water if diffracted; if it was hard radiation it condensed. Acids fought with alkalis. There was a time and a place. They could hear themselves sweat.

When Paradine reached the edge of the cliffs, he turned and called; "Come." Helena fell beside him; Kraag beat blindly at the air; further behind, Merganser tore away the last of his beautiful clothes. But they all entered into the golden forest where the tall feathery trees towered over them, making a bronze

38

twilight. As they lay beneath the trees, the sound of their breath was like oceans.

"Is it?" said Merganser. "A place? Here?"

"No," laboured Paradine. "Instability. Total."

Helena touched one of the trees. "They're gentle," she said.

"Look," said Kraag. He dragged himself to his feet, his great paws dangling at his sides, a man in rags, and turned his bald head up to bronze light. "I've seen. Rain?"

A cloud of darkness swept down and came threshing through the golden trees. It rushed past and swept in again, a golden cloud quilted on the underside like lakes of tar, and with obsidian claws. They turned to run, but the great golden paw swept down once again, and the golden head of the suntyke slewed round to gnash at them with teeth of lightnings. It was

sunset. To right and left, as far as eye could see, the main squadrons stretched in level flight, until they disappeared into the twilight haze on each flank. Squadron by squadron, company by company, the huge birds cruised steadily through the air, their wings moving in perfect unison, their plumage glowing like copper, their cruel golden eyes staring at nothing, their great yellow beaks thrust out like rams. Far below them across the scarlet fleece of clouds, the light-armed scouts swooped and whirled.

Merganser glanced proudly to left and right along the lines of his first full command, a veteran colonel of the Free Cavalry, the oldest and proudest warrior race in this universe. Slowly he raised his falchion, and all along the line, to right and left, tiny riders mounted on each bird raised their pennoned lances in salute, and their armour glowed points of phosphorescent blue in the twilight.

This was how the Free People lived, always aloft above the cloud-layer on their unresting birds, with whom they lived in a delicate symbiotic balance which had evolved in the long forgotten ages since they took to the air to avoid the wreck of their planet. They lived, bred and died on the backs of the birds; and the birds themselves lived always on the wing, carrying their young in pouches until they were fledged. Their world was a perpetual cloudscape, and they knew nothing of what lay below; there was the land of the dead, the great deep into which dead bird and dead man were cast.

In daylight they slept, the birds dozing on the wing, while the whiteness dazzled below. In broad starlight they gathered for festivals, the pipes and quill-harps harmonising to the drumming cries of the birds and the choirs of shrill voices. Or they sailed in procession among the solemn towers of cloud, or circled among curtains of vapour in the mysteries of the nuptial flight, swooping down to draw back and embody the ancestral spirits from the land of the dead. They dreaded the perilous upthrust of storms, which they placated with sacrifices; they rode the swooping currents of the jet-streams. But the favourite time of the People was the long, slow evening, when they rode the sunset line, and foraged, and were convivial. It was the human time between the blinding noon and the spirit-haunted starlight, when by preference they travelled like this, with the screen of Free Cavalry thrust out ahead to guard against enemies— drifters, mutated bats, avioids—and scout for new feeding-grounds.

The cloud-floor tumbled away below them, and they entered into a broad valley, as fine as they had ever seen, its towering walls all rose and ash and amber in the evening sun. The shining floor was sparkled thickly with ripe air-spores, on which, as far as eye could see, dark droves of skimmers browsed. There was food and prey there for generations of the People. Perhaps if a stasis could be achieved, they would remain there forever, circling in this good place, and he would become High Chief and have many wives.

As the line of great birds bunched and swept out across the valley, he glanced back and saw the People swooping over the cloud-ridge behind him. A thousand points of blue fire flashed in the dusk in salute and greeting.

A shrill cry from the left brought him around quickly. At first it seemed that the evening sun had multiplied itself; and then he saw that great globes of metal were rising up out of the vapour on both sides of the valley, and shining blood-red in the sun.

He had barely time to shout the order to wheel about when the first bolt seared across the valley, striking across the flank, and the clouds shook with thunder. Bolt after bolt followed, and the great birds, maddened with fear, swirled and fought and collided. Clouds of skimmers swarmed up to blind them. Twisting about, clinging desperately to the harness, he saw that other rows of the globes had risen behind and among the People, and great chains of lightning twisted and leapt among them. The birds fell, blind and burning, and the lost riders flashed blue as they tumbled screaming into the clouds.

Stronger birds beat desperately upwards until they collapsed and plunged back, bringing new ruin among them. One such, he saw, fell down shrieking among the globes and struck one which collapsed in thunder, a great balloon of metal foil. He might yet save what was left of the People, though he would never lead them now. Calling to his bodyguard, who still swooped about him, he brought them into a ragged line and wheeled left into the rank of globes. Others riders caught the idea, and one, two globes burst and sank as the birds' great beaks rammed home. The range shortened, but too late, and the lightnings arced harmlessly over them; but the enemy only now showed themselves. From the cloud wall drove a wedge of glittering metal machines and the goggled fliers swept them like scythes through the thinning ranks of birds. He had no time to know that, forgotten ages ago, there had been other accommodations, other ways of refuge, other evolutions.

A machine dived down at him, keening in the thin air. For a moment he saw, close and clear, the pilot's naked body shining with a thin film of oil, the masked face grinning at him. Then his bird screamed and

41

side-slipped, one wing torn off by the glancing impact of the machine. Weeping for his lost Kingdom he tumbled down, and the floor of the cloud-valley split open, and he fell towards the burning surface of the dead planet a hundred leagues below.

rock. He knew the rock and tasted it with all his senses. He lived with the harsh taste of basalt, the sweet-sourness of metallic ores, the blandness of oil-shales, the crusted saltiness of diluvian tracts, the light crumbling richness of organic deposits. It was his element, in which he lived, moving slowly among its endless caverns, gulfs and fissures.

Kraag, like all his kind, was a solitary. Except for the bleak brief matings which maintained his sparse race, he had no intimate contact with the others, for like him they lived in a state of perpetual mineral wonder. Sometimes two would sit together for a while, squat limbs working as they conveyed in guttural sounds the qualities and textures they had experienced. Then one would reach out to taste or touch, and they would drift away, tasting, touching, slowly sensing out the changing textures of their world.

It was an immediate world, in which the tastes combined into a complicated ever-renewed pattern. He could dimly remember being a young one, as a time when the pattern was simple, and each sensation was new. And he was aware that the old ones slowly ceased to wander, settled in some favoured spot and at last became one with it. He found them occasionally; they crumbled richly.

Once, during his middle times, when life was most zestful and wandering widest, he found an old one, and spoke with it. It was one of the other ones, the mates, but too old, yet alive in a curious way. It lived in a cavern near a volcanic vent, and the very air was full of the pungent peppery scent of fire and rock.

Good here, said the old one. Stand and taste. Strong. Good.

Stand. Taste, said Kraag. Good.

42

Old, said the old one. Old tastes weak. Wants strong strong taste. Sharp. Hot. Rich.

Rich, said Kraag. Old one good good.

The old one rasped its touchers to show pleasure, and offered him a small nodule of jade. He found it excellent, and said so. This was followed by other politenesses, the old one meanwhile tasting pumice, and gradually it began to talk.

A past thing. A mate. Tasting, talking. It knew. A big wandering. Beyond the fire. A long cavern. Many fissures. Much water falling. Cliffs: long small cavern. Still water. Under water. Caverns of poor tasteless sand. Up a crevice. A place, air moving. Many tastes, faint, unknown. Fear fear fear. Down and back. Here.

Kraag felt the fear. Air moving, he said. Unknown tastes. No good thing.

The mate wanted wanted, much wanted, said the old one. Wandered. Not known.

He stood there, his body tingling with the intoxicating spiced taste of the fire, and his mind slowly turned over these new things. It disturbed him deeply, the way the old one not only remembered, but recalled another's memory and tried to pass on acquired knowledge. Even worse was the memory itself, of the purposeful journey and of the air that moved and tasted of fear. Yet as he chewed on it his mind, stimulated by the fiery scent, took hold, and the thing became so new, so tasty in his mind, that it drew all his sense towards it. It filled him with dim wonder, that something in his mind tasted more real than rock.

After a long time he took a piece of the pumice to calm himself, and said, Want. Going. Climb. New thing.

No, said the old one, no. Mate went. Not known.

Going, said Kraag. Here good. Old one good. Going.

And with a touch he went slowly towards the fiery scent. Thus began Kraag's journey, which he told of to others whom he met on the way so that it became a legend in the caverns, passing slowly from one to another, always dimmer and less communicable, until it died away into the rock.

Passing the fire was both pleasant and terrible. He felt his way along a narrow ledge which led up and down beside the fire-pit, and the intoxication of the fire made the rocks slip and stagger. Several times he swayed over, but always the reassurance of the rock-wall drew him back and its touch cleared his head. When at last he came out into the broad cavern beyond, his treaders seemed to be going different ways, and he grunted meaninglessly and waved his touchers about. Then he tripped on a stone, his mind darkened as it did after mating, and he lay still for a number of times.

When he began to move again, he felt confused, and his sensations were overlaid by the new things which the old one had put into his mind. He touched and tasted distractedly, and wandered for many times, pushing as far as he could into the crevices, which always ended in blank walls, or forked and petered out. Others lived there, but they began to fear him, and one began to make the fighting noises at him, so that he went away, because the other was young and strong.

His stumbling flight took him far along a new crevice, and here, refreshing himself, he sensed a heavy vibration in the rock. Following it, he came at last to an open place, and the air was full of water falling past him to somewhere far below. There were climbing-rocks beside the water, and he dragged himself up them for a very long way. Water splashed over him continuously, so that he felt cold and heavy, and everything was tasteless. But at last he reached the top, and left the water, and passed through the long narrow cavern where he moved with difficulty, sometimes lying down, but the rock was very good.

By now, as each thing became real, the old one's memories of memories possessed him completely. He found the still water, and went down into it, under the rock-wall, and came out chill and weak on the other side. He fed after a fashion on the poor dull sand, until he came to the crevice where the rock was strange. As he tasted it, the air started to move. He felt old with fear, but he would follow it, so that he could go back and say it all to the old one and the fighting one and the others.

The tastes in the air were strange and feeble; when he reached down and picked up the small things that lay thickly about the ground, they were mushy. But a great air blew towards him, and with all his will he moved into it, until suddenly, he knew, there was no more cavern about him. Instead, the air was filled with heat and something more, a force so voluminous sustained and violent that it streamed through his whole body, transforming it. Here at last was, not rock, but the rock-maker. Fire, he said, all. The last thing he knew was the taste of his own body, sweet and sour, fruity yet unsatisfying. In the grey waste, the sun glared down upon a single rock, and the mirages began to dance.

blankets. They filled the whole of the long corrugated iron hut, neatly folded and stacked, row upon row, from floor to ceiling. At various times during the day, heavy trucks would come crunching in low gear down the road of clinker and loose scoria, and from each one the driver and his mate would unload piles of used blankets, matted, sour, sweaty from much use. These were carefully piled on one side, near the double-door. Then he would issue an exactly equivalent number of new or cleaned blankets, crisp, fluffy, sharp with the smell of DDT; and having counted them twice, he made out the appropriate receipts in triplicate, one copy for the depot, one for the driver, one for himself. If additional blankets were required, these could be issued only against a voucher signed by an officer of appropriate seniority. All his files and ledgers were neatly kept on a trestle table in the corner, from which, every evening, his accounts with their supporting receipts and vouchers were handed to a despatch rider, who took them to the base-depot, in an envelope marked URGENT. Every Friday afternoon the trucks from depot took away the sour-smelling used blankets; every Monday the same trucks brought new or cleaned ones.

It made a simple but satisfying life for Paradine.

Somewhere, he knew, over the horizon the Thousand Years War rumbled on; sometimes, by day, aircraft drummed overhead, and at night distant flashes which were not lightning flickered against the clouds from below the skyline. Convoys of trucks passed to and fro along the main road to the staging-camp up on the hill, bring singing men on draft from the base, returning with silent men on leave from the front. Each convoy stopped for the night at the staging camp, and each man was given a hot supper, a shower, a wooden bed and three blankets to sleep on, and in the morning breakfast and a haversack ration. Then they went their opposite ways, the leave men singing, the draft men silent. He watched them come and go without curiosity; he assumed that, like the blankets, they would be adequately covered by receipts and vouchers.

It was always raining, except when, once in a while, a watery sun blinked through a gap in the overcast. The clay road to the store was churned into creamy mud by the trucks, but once a week other trucks came with fatigue parties and spread loads of clinker and scoria, which became slowly pounded into the mud. Three times a day he would take off his slippers, put on his gumboots, poncho and rainhat, lock the doors, cross the duckboards to the road and trudge up the hill to the big steaming mess-hall, where he ate. At the long tables, eating their bacon-sandwiches, or duff, or corned beef fritters, were the men who had stopped over from the truck convoys, the wild- or weary-eyed men on leave and the new recruits who liked to sit near them, and find out how bad it was going to be up there.

A man would say; "Hill 49, that wasn't too good. It was a salient, see, and it overlooked our trenches for miles, and they said we had to take it to straighten out the line. Told us it would be all right too, a cakewalk, with corps artillery, bomber support, new heavy tanks, the lot. Well, we got there, some of us, what didn't get hung up on the wire, or caught in the crossfire from the flank, or cut up by our own barrage. The bombers hit the wrong hill, and most of the tanks got mudded. But quite a lot of us got to the top, it wasn't too bad. Then they hit us with everything, all we had and more, and their bombers didn't miss, and their tanks got through, and then they come round the hill, not over it, but round both sides at the bottom. So we pulled out, what was left, and three of us was stuck in a shell-hole for three days, with a young officer hit in the guts and crying for water. Lucky he died, we couldn't have carried him. So we come back."

"That's enough, soldier," growled a grey-haired corporal, settling himself at the end of the table. "You know the rules about loose talk and spreading alarm and despondency."

"That's what I say, corp," said the soldier cheerfully. "It could've been worse. I seen a lot worse . . . Don't you want those sausages, mate? Ta, I'll finish them for you."

There were other storemen too, silent men like himself. They worked in other long huts that dealt in such merchandise as greatcoats, webbing-equipment and portable latrines. Sometimes they talked among themselves, slowly and quietly, and mostly about their trades, comparing for example, the seasonal fluctuation in number of blankets issued with that for messtins or artillery plotting-tables. But they preferred to sit, austere and a little apart, listening to the endlessly-renewed conversation of the transients, or in the canteen of an evening, drinking weak beer while the others sang sentimental songs.

Paradine did not patronise the canteen very often, much preferring the cosy retreat he had contrived in the far corner of the store-hut. There he had built up the stacks of blankets to make a dividing wall, and had made a couch of blankets, on which he would lie with new fluffy blankets warmly tucked about him. With a mug of cold tea and his cigarettes beside him, and the petrol-lamp hissing, he could lie as snugly as an ancient emperor, listening to the Forces Programme on the radio, half washed-out by static, and reading comic-books and picture-magazines supplied by Army Comforts. Or, more and more often, he would lie back and stare up into the cathedral-like darkness of the roof, while the piles of blankets towered above him as permanent as stone, and the everlasting rain drummed on the roof.

On Sundays, when the store was closed, he sometimes dozed there all day, except for meals. These were the times when he had strange dreams, of great birds that fell blazing from the sky, of rocks walking in the desert, of steam-engines that crashed together and screamed in enormous fury . . .

One Monday morning, after the truck from depot had delivered a load of clean blankets, Paradine was seated at his desk making up the vouchers. The driver, spattered with yellow mud like his truck, stood by the open door smoking a tab-end and staring out at the rain.

"Not much, is it?" he said disparagingly.

"I dunno," said Paradine, "it's a life."

"You mean to say we're alive?"

"It's not my idea of heaven, mate."

"Who said anything about heaven?"

wind. All night long the dry hot wind out of the plains blew with steady fury, and she bent and strained beneath it. Around her, in the fitful flashes of light, she could see others twisting, with tossing limbs, and she could hear the tearing screech of the wind about them. At first the wind had been full of debris, dust, small stones, leaves, branches, but even these were now gone; anything moveable had been swept away, and there was nothing but straining shapes and bare earth and the noise of the wind. Behind that mindless roaring, she could sense the movement and feeling of the others, not articulated or imaged, simply a continuous fluctuating drone of endurance and panic.

Then there was something else too, something very bitter. The old one, the mother who had dropped them all, stood on top of the hill, dry and withered, but still tall. Like the others, Helena could sense in her own being the last pulses of despair and resignation from the dim old mind, and the inward wrench as the tall shape finally toppled and fell crackling to the ground.

The wind died out with the night, and in the cool dawn she could see the other dendroids, all rooted about the hill, all, like her, in disarray, stripped of leaf and bud, dry as tinder. There would be no young that season. Not far away, its last flickers of consciousness extinguished, lay the trunk of the old one, split apart and revealing its pitiful hollowness.

In a sudden hiss of steam, a green locomotive came over the hill. The wood-burners had not fed for days, and had some sense which drew them to fallen dendroids. This one drew up slowly to the felled trunk and waited, puffing excitedly, before it swung broadside on and drove its scoop along the shattered side. All the people sighed and shivered. The scoop flung out a shower of splintered wood which was picked up in the hopper and ingested. After another pause to rebuild its falling head of steam, the engine tootled merrily, and was answered from nearby.

Three more of the machine-creatures came over the hill, two of them simple wood-burners like the first, but the third a modified traction-engine with a portable chain-saw extension. It settled itself beside the mutilated trunk, and the others waited expectantly with lowered scoops. The sunlight glittered on the delicate web of the self-operating controls in the cab of each machine, the small gears turning, the miniature pistons releasing tiny jets of steam. The chainsaw ripped down and down, quartering the old body, and presently, with excited hissings and hootings, they all began to feed.

The dendroids swayed and shivered, ashamed yet glad that the saws and scoops were tearing at the desecrated trunk of the mother, and not at them; yet they were afraid, knowing that where some fed, others would come and be less fastidious.

Helena painfully averted her senses towards the plain. A herd of small slow tank-engines clanked up out of the gulley where the stream ran low. Spattered with grey mud, but with full tanks, they began to browse slowly along the plain, ripping up the starved turf and intaking the soft coal underneath. They puffed and chuckled; high overhead, a flock of winged shapes fled screaming across the pitiless sun. Acrid smoke lay thick on the parched air.

The racial memories in which she shared carried images of a green time when the dendroids and lesser beings had possessed the earth, spreading slowly, age by age, their peaceful communities, sleeping through the long winters, waking to new life and the solemn endless participation in one another's being. Then, so briefly that it could hardly be recalled, much less defined, something had lived among them, a small thing that moved its limbs freely about the ground. When it left, the others came, steaming, clanking, gouging, coal-burners, wood-burners, great predators, filling the groves with smoke and clatter, tearing down, scarifying the grass. The hot winds had come, and the people of the dendroids had shrunk to scattered dying communities like this one. Their shared dream, with which they comforted themselves in the bitter winters, was that someday the thing which had walked across the ground would return, and all the steamers would go away.

One of the browsing tankers suddenly began to hoot in alarm. The rest swung about sensing. Across the plain came a distant screaming whistle, a sound of fear, knife-edged and triumphant, growing louder as it came. Out of the dust haze, its pistons driving, its single light glaring, terrible with bell and whistle, came one of the great predators. The small tankers scattered in blind panic, and the wood-burners drew together defensively among the chips and sawdust of the dismembered mother.

The predator drove straight at the oldest and largest of the tankers, which clanked and fussed in useless movement, its worn bearings clattering as it tried to escape into the grove. The predator smashed it ruthlessly against the base of one of the dendroids; the great hollow steel fangs flashed out, and there was a dreadful gurgling and scraping as the broken body was rifled of its fuel and water. Without pause, the killer swung about and crushed another victim.

Into Helena's mind came a shrill soundless cry of alarm. There was a new smell in the air, and from the crushed side of the first tanker, where it rested against the tall dendroid, thin streamers of smoke began to appear. Scattered embers were already burning into the parched wood; a long ragged flame leapt up and blazed among the stripped branches. A puff of wind blew it upward into a crackling torch; they could all feel the heat of it, and the screaming now almost destroyed the mind. The wind strengthened, whipping the tall trunks about, and the fire flashed across the grove in a single disastrous blast, as if the wind itself had turned to flame. The engines clattered about dementedly under a rain of blazing branches; the express, having taken its fill, shrieked on into the distance. She was aware at last only of the common agony and despair, as the trunks fell and crashed onto a general pyre, under which a trapped tanker hooted continuously.

Birds fell from the air. Rock crumbled. Landscape slowly dissolved in the downpour. Ash whirled up in a pillar of flame. The instability shifted, and the matrix became strictly binary.

FOUR

MARTIN IRONBENDER 11212 leaned forward over the wheel of his jetcar, and looked cautiously about. The long straight road through the housing estate, bordered by shrubs and low hedges, was quite empty, and well away from the towers of flats; there were no helicars or hoverers in the air. His hand reached out stealthily to the instrument-panel.

Mr. Ironbender had the bland reliable manner appropriate to a conveyancer in the Debatable Lands Development Corporation; but his secret drama was the life of the old-time dragsters in the trideo shows. He dreamed of them as he idled from client to client at the wheel of the robot-controlled jetcar. At rare times, when there was no one about, he would press the switch which disconnected the car from the protective web of scanners and buried cables, set it on manual, and for a few moments, he was Reddy McGurk, king of the dragsters, hero of the video stories of olden times.

Over the hedge at the roadside, a scarlet paraball tumbled in slow and irregular flight, and after it a skinny boy, all arms and legs, landed with a flying leap in the road. For an instant of no-time, nothing happened. Mr. Ironbender, hand poised over the control panel, stared out at the boy—the tousled head, the mouth agape with instant terror. The boy Seth stared at the white shocked face of the driver who glared at him through the vision-screen. Then the time-lines divided, both man and boy were aware of a fleeting sense of duplication, and two equal and opposite things happened, thus maintaining the balance of forces in the universe.

(Martin Ironbender 11212 swung the wheel and fumbled for the powerbrake button and missed it by a finger's breadth. The front buffer caught Seth 1 and tossed him over the roof of the jetcar, leaving a bright smear of blood on the vision-screen. Mr. Ironbender pulled in to the verge and was sick, while, summoned by the automatic alarm, the blue police hoverer and the white ambulance helivan dropped out of the sky. Seth 1's time-line, and all the other time-lines that might have stemmed from it, aborted as he died on the concrete. Ironbender received five years corrective detention plus permanent suspension of license for major traffic infraction, lost a ruinous suit for criminal damages, and spent a lifetime of drudgery as legman for Universal Pollsters).

Martin Ironbender 112122 punched the automatic emergency button, and the robot's reactions, ten thousand times faster than his own, sent the jetcar careering into a shrieking S-turn which missed the boy by centimeters. Leaving it all to the robot, then and forever, Mr. Ironbender lay back sickly in his seat, and reached for a tranko pill from the dispenser. He went on in later life to become either the Fifteenth Veep of the DLDC, or winner of third prize in the Grand Asteroid Confederation Lottery, which made him too rich for his own good and either caused his wife to leave him, or not.

Seth 2 panted and shivered and stared after the jetcar as it disappeared down the quiet suburban road. Then he carefully crossed the road, retrieved the scarlet paraball which had lodged in the hedge, and went back to his solitary complex game at the electric volleyboard.

The examination-machines in the open booths hummed and clicked softly. Seth 2, taking the second battery of college-entrance tests, leaned back and watched as the screen cleared and filled again with the next question. It read:

Elganif's Proposition states that
  (1) *Since all things are possible, the will is free.*
  (2) *Since the will is free, all things are possible.*
  (3) *If all things are possible, the will is free.*
  (4) *If the will is free, all things are possible.*

As his finger hesitated over the push-buttons, there came once again the almost imperceptible stasis, the sense of doubleness, the bifurcation of the time-lines.

(Seth 221121 pressed button number 1, and continued with the remainder of the tests. By the end of the afternoon, his score came out of the computer at 191.2 BX, and he was assigned to the Faculty of Descriptive Sciences, where he majored in geology.

The time-lines divided. Dr. Seth Paradine 2211211 was appointed to the faculty and began the climb up towards academic success, becoming in the end either a celebrated prizeman or a traitor.

Seth 2211212 migrated south and became an oil-prospector, and either died poor and in great misery, or acquired an immense fortune).

Seth 221122 pressed button number 3, and continued with the remainder of the tests. When he finished, the machinery clicked and gobbled for several seconds before spitting out a plasticard from the delivery-slot. It read:

> *Your score is 178.6 BK*
> *You are assigned to the School of Business Management*
> *Report for interview at 0920 hours tomorrow to Dr. Buglehorn, Block C, Room 51.*
> *The Board of Examiners wishes you success in your studies.*

Dr. Seth Paradine 221122121 stared down briefly from the window of his office on the thirty-ninth floor, watching the tiny buzzcars creeping along the multiways far below and the sunlight gleaming on the long reach of the harbour, finely streaked with the wakes of hovercraft. Across the room, the day's prices were beginning to trickle continuously in fiery letters across the information board:

> ... Elangful Koords 36.2 ... Predge Incorporated 5.7 ... Breakages Limited 101.5 ... Treef and Treef Debentures 77.8 ... Agarble Futures 17.7 ... Bird/Feather Associates 67.3 ... Mount Axorax Mining 42.3 ... Bdurbian Rails 17.9 ...

Associated Enterprise Holdings 13.4 ... Rock-bottom Insurance 50.5 ...

Satisfied that the world was proceeding normally, he sat down at his desk, a young KRASCO executive almost out of probation, and confident in his independent assignment. He turned a page of his notes and spoke into the dictotype; the machine chittered softly as it translated the vocables into typescript. The shadow of a passenger-flitter flicked across the room, and for a moment his eyes turned towards the window and his mind to the world outside. A tall tower of cloud was building up on the horizon. The fiery symbols continued to trickle silently down the board:

    ... Base Metals Developments 42.2 ... Dinkum Oil 97.7 ... Things Incorporated 29.6 ... Ftoomian Nargostics 7.4 ...
Stasis. Doubleness. Bifurcation.

(Seth 2211221211 watched the towering cloud, and returned satisfied to the conclusion of his report:
"We would therefore conclude with confidence that Ftoomian Nargostics is a development stock with significant and sound possibilities, which might well be included in the standard investor's portfolio."
He pressed the release button and the sheets slid onto his desk. When they had been corrected, he fed them back into the machine, rechecked his final copy, signed it, and dropped it into the transfer slot.
The junior executive's lunchroom was fairly full, but he found a quiet corner table and dialled for cold seafood, salad and cheese. Just as the tray slid out from the wall-slot, Bill Merganser eased himself into the opposite seat. He wore the same dark suit as Paradine, the same house-tie, but whereas on Paradine it had the look of a uniform, Merganser's pale hair and pink eyes gave him an air of benignity and joy.
"Hello, Seth, seafood, eh? I think I'll just stick to coffee. Must keep the mind clear this afternoon. How's your report going?"

"Fine," said Paradine, savouring a prawn. "Just put it down the slot."

Merganser raised his colourless eyebrows. "So soon? What a little executive it is. At least I'll be able to say: I knew him once, he passed me on the way up."

"Mustn't jump to conclusions," said Paradine stiffly. "How's yours going?"

"Oh that thing—not even on the dicto yet. But I'm still waiting for a bit more material ... I say, have you seen Number One's daughter? She was in his office this morning—got the most astronomical legs, and her figure—breep ..."

He chattered on about girls and riverside dancehalls and hoverboard skating, and seemed to look with pleasure on Paradine, who was smugly daydreaming about the report which would be lying on Number One's desk after lunch.

"You take entire responsibility for this report?" said Kraag. On him, the dark uniform suit, of finer cloth and tailoring, only served to bring out the brutality of the big face, whose hard mouth and cavernous nostrils were reflected upside down in the finely-polished surface of the desk.

"Yes, indeed, Mr. Kraag," said Paradine with the right tone of modest assurance.

"And your recommendation is entirely favourable?"

"Yes, Mr. Kraag."

"Did you investigate the connection with Aquamines Limited?"

"Not—not in depth, Mr. Kraag."

"Not in depth?"

"The connection was slight, Mr. Kraag, and I thought ..."

"You incompetent gibbering gruck, you *can't* think," roared Kraag in sudden awful wrath, and the desk clanked beneath his fist. "It's the key to the whole sorry mess. If you'd bothered to check the individual holdings, you'd have found that through a carefully-covered series of interlocking preemptions, Aquamines control the residuary mineral rights which are Ftoomian Nargostics' only real asset. Without that, they're

56

just a phoney corporation doing a big trade in non-existent commodities."

Paradine stared at the swollen reflection of Kraag's face on the polished desk, and muttered:

"I'm sorry, Mr. Kraag, if you'd allow me to recheck . . ."

"Fortunately I've saved you that trouble," said Kraag pleasantly, and into the intercom: "Mr. Merganser, please."

The door opened almost at once, and Merganser entered, benign and joyful.

"Yes, Mr. Kraag?"

"Mr. Merganser, tell Mr. Paradine the news."

"You mean about Aquamines, Mr. Kraag?"

"No, no," said Kraag impatiently, "he knows that—now. Tell him the morning news."

"Ftoomian Nargostics dropped forty points overnight. Aquamines pulled away the props, and the roof fell in."

Kraag flipped over the report and scrawled a decisive mark on it, which Paradine knew was a rejection.

"But Mr. Kraag—please—my career . . ."

"It's finished," said Kraag, "with us. That's the rule—no mistakes—none. I suggest you apply to the Test Centre for relocation in a job where mistakes are allowed. Pick up your card on the way out."

As Seth Paradine 221122121 walked to the door, he knew that their eyes watched him, sardonic and contemptuous.

The Centre relocated him for training as an art historian, there being few other available candidates. After graduating, he became either a successful art critic or a celebrated art-thief; in this capacity he either did or did not carry off the last and most beautiful of Fioredespina's tactiles, after which he may, or may not, have disappeared.)

Seth 2211221212 turned away from the window and caught the flicker of fiery symbols on the board: . . . Ftoomian Nargostics 7.4 . . . A forty-point drop overnight; he must have missed something big. That odd link with Aquamines was something he'd never followed up; if he took a wakey-pill and worked all

57

night, he could still have it on Number One's desk by the time he came in tomorrow morning.

Kraagshaven was not so much a great house as a sumptuous village, which dropped down the hillside in a series of terraces and arcades, stairways and winding ramps, halls, towers, balconies and service-rooms, to where the dark waters of the bay lapped on beaches and jetties. Even the closing curve of the bay belonged to Kraag and was tamed; a bubble-curtain in the mouth of the bay broke the waves, and the small island was a radar-station for the hydrofoils and amphibian helicraft. The terraces were warmed underfoot, and protected by wind deflectors from the autumn gale. Only the cold stars overhead, and the driving cloudwrack, could not be tamed, but they could be comfortably ignored.

"My father's a strange man, stranger than you know," said Helena Kraag.

"He's a perfectionist," said Paradine, "that's strange, in business."

"No mistakes?"

"Not one. He's generous, but pitiless."

They walked moodily along the wide deserted terrace, while a complicated minor dance-rhythm pattered away in the distance. He wore the new dark evening kit with the exaggeratedly wide shoulders and the thin tapering trousers; walking beside him, trying to match his long slow strides, the girl in her filmy dress gleamed faintly in the starlight, like the phosphorescence out beyond the bay.

"Isn't everyone?"

"Not everyone. No one's like him; that's why he's very rich."

"Oh, rich, yes, but there's other things ... Did you know he designed all this? Bought out a small fishing town to do it. He'd like to do that for a city, for a country."

"Kraagopolis. Kraagland ... I say, who's that watching over there?"

"Where? I can't see anyone."

"By the stairway. It looks like ... no ..."

58

"Don't be weird," she said. "No one's tnere."

"I could have sworn . . ."

Paradine shrugged and turned his long saturnine face to the sea. Far off, the exhaust of an intercontinental rocket showed briefly, like a meteor sliding back into the sky.

"You know what we're all here for tonight?" she said leading him towards a rambling stairway, which they climbed side by side.

"To announce the new vice-president?"

"Yes, everyone knows that. But what they don't know is that I shall also marry him."

Paradine stopped near the top of the stairs. "You mean—he really wants to run it like one of those old kings, doesn't he? Daughter, I give thee this man for husband. Haven't you any pride?"

She slipped her hand into his, and led him out onto a balcony which leaned out over a toppling cliff of buildings, with the sea below.

"Very few people know this," she said, "and no one knows the real secret. I do the choosing. Only you know that."

"I never thought that Kraag . . ."

"But don't you see? I must marry the heir apparent, to keep it all in the family. Plenty of bright young men could take over the business really, it's all a matter of training. So he let's me pick the one I want. I tell you, he's great and strange."

She was standing very close to him, her lips almost touching his. "It could be you," she murmured, "I'd like it to be you."

There was a disordered shriek from behind them; her eyes went wide with fear, and she pressed close against him, hiding her face against his throat. A sea-bird, diving into the violent uprush of air from the deflectors, was flung aloft, fluttered and fell back screaming, to be tossed aloft again, tumbling over and over, shrieking with rage and terror. Some minor ingenuity of radar went into action, there was a faint cough, and the bird dissolved into a cloud of feathers which flickered in the window-lights, and blew away. So one was caught, raised up, blundered, blew away.

59

"Is it gone?" she said, raising her head and brushing back her heavy bright hair.

"The zappies got it," said Paradine. She shivered in his arms.

"You know," she said, slipping an arm around his neck, "we're alike, we two. We could work together." She kissed him. "Even kings grow old, and then there'd be us. Please? . . . please?" The word doubled, echoed, in a brief stillness of untime. Then—

Seth 22112212122 said, "Darling, I'm very fond of you, but . . ."

Seth 22112212121 pulled her body close against his, and began to kiss her. The deflected gale beat up behind them like muffled drums.

Later, as he stood in the shimmering glass ballroom, with Kraag's heavy hand on his shoulder, and Helena at his side, and all the guests applauding, all he could see in the end was Billy Merganser's pale face, beneath the pale hair, collapsing into despair and rage.

(Seth Paradine 22112212122 remained a bachelor and had various affairs, each of which drifted him onto a different time-line. In all of them except one [in which he was accidentally gunned down by a cop named Ironbender during the Great Heliport Stick-up] he became eleventh vice-president of KRASCO. As time went on, he bifurcated less and less, and, in the end, not at all.)

As the luxurious executive-flitter locked onto the island beacon, a soft bell-note sounded. Seth Paradine 22112212121 finished reading the summary, slipped the plastic sheets back into his briefcase and sealed it. That was the last of it. Kraag's attorneys had provided craftily for the estate duties, and his financial empire had passed almost intact to his daughter and her husband. Paradine touched his eyelids lightly with his fingertips, and felt the faint wrinkles at the corners of the eyes. He was still a young man, with many years before him, and it was all his—KRASCO, Kraagshaven, Helena . . . Life was very good. He leaned back and sipped his medicated brandy and soda.

He had set the window-filters high to keep out the glare of the setting sun, and the landscape flowed past beneath him in tones of grey, like the old bioscope-films he had seen in the university museums. Ahead, the squat landward towers of Kraagshaven humped up against a dull sea, the outer bastions which guarded the inner maze, growing more intricate year by year, of airy rooms and pleasure-courts and unexpected alcoves.

Something flickered like fine louvres in front of the flowing grey landscape. He fingered his tired eyelids. When he opened them again, the flicker had stopped; something, someone, stood there in the cabin of the flitter. It was a man, as tall as himself, taller perhaps, very thin, dressed in the rags of a tropical cool-suit, useless, its vac-tank gone. He had difficulty in focusing the face; there was an impression of unkempt hair, a beard, a gaping mouth, and fierce puffy eyes. The hand gestured towards the cracked swollen mouth and then almost touched the cool-misted brandy glass. As never before, he felt his whole body prickle with sudden horror; the eyes, swimming into focus, were the same that stared out at him every morning and evening from the reversal-mirror as his barber-masseur groomed him. A long way off, the glass dashed on the floor; the flitter dropped down into the lights of the landing-pad, and he was alone. But the disturbing presence remained with him through the brief ride in the subway-shuttle; through the session with Aino the barber-masseur, the powerful spatulate fingers caressing his temples; through the long leisurely dinner of seafood eaten on a tall balcony cantilevered out over the sea, with the house-guests laughing and cheering each time a sea-bird was zappied into a cloud of feathers, out beyond the air-curtain; until at last it walked back into his dreams.

He awoke suddenly, and sat up on his sleeping-couch, soaked in sweat, his mouth dry, pasty, foul-tasting. His first thought was that the controls must have gone wrong; but the usual blanket of warm, lightly moistened air continued to wash gently over his body, and a glass of chilled fruit-juice appeared when he touched the autoserve. The light was strange. The rear wall of the long oval room blurred away into a harsh blaze of sunlight and a landscape of rock and dust. Walking over to it, he saw a ragged figure crouched by the rock, patiently holding a tin against a small darkened fissure that might be a seepage. When it sensed his presence, it rose to its feet, dropping the tin with a clatter, and walked to meet him, and he saw it, the same, with his own terror looking at him out of his own eyes.

They met and passed through each other, like a breath, and he walked on into the little dry canyon. There was the rag of a tent there, and a dead burro, unburied, and a few poor survey-instruments scattered on a flat rock. There was a dreadful scent of dry decay, and many large flies; the heat flowed over him like a thick liquid. The thirst was now merciless; his swollen tongue filled his parched mouth. There was only the rusty tin, and the small fissure in the rock, dark with a promise of moisture. He knelt and pressed his lips to it, and drew back with a croak of pain as the alkali burnt his swollen tongue.

The top-lights glowed on. He was still sitting up on his couch with the glass of orange-juice untasted in his hand and the warm air washing around his body and the sweat streaming down his back.

"That was a hell of a noise," said Helena. She came walking from her couch at the far end of the long oval room, drawing the filmy folds of a thermocloak around her sun-tanned nakedness. "You scared me, sweetie. You made a noise, a scary noise, choking, like a dying man." She sat on the end of the couch, not touching him, and looked at him calculatingly.

"I had a dream," he said. "I suppose I did. I'm not sure, it was so real. Look how I'm sweating."

She nodded at the glass in his hand. "Tried a dozy pill?"

He shook his head. "It's not like that," he said. "It wasn't like a dream." He reached towards her, in a sudden gesture asking for help, like the ragged man

62

reaching out for the glass. "Something else happened on the way home, in the flitter. It didn't seem like sleep, but I suppose it was."

She looked at him, making no move. "Perhaps you'd better see a psychman," she said. "Billy Merganser knows a good one."

"Billy need a psychman?" he said. The idea was new to him, and took a little of the edge off his dream.

"Oh," she said, "yes. For a long time, ever since our engagement party, he says." She patted his knee perfunctorily. "Take a dozy-pill, sweetie, and I'll get you an appointment tomorrow. I'm going back to my couch. You know where to find me—if you want me." She drifted off down the room in the cloud of her thermocloak, and he watched her over the rim of the chilled glass, and felt the sweat drying on his body.

But he did not want her, and he did not want a dozy-pill. He lay awake, staring into the dark. He had made his life, and even in those vague moments of hesitation, had taken the right choices. Helena, Kraagshaven, KRASCO—it had all come his way until Kraag died, and then it had changed. Helena had needed him, desperately, as an ally against her formidable father. With his death (the collapsing figure in the boardroom seemed curiously vague and ambiguous in recollection) it had changed. Helena, with her hard mind and lifelong knowledge of the firm, could stand alone. He could become merely a mate, a drone. Life was shifting; he was no longer in control.

When the first streaks of day paled across the tall arched window, he rose from the sleeping-couch and slipped on his swimbriefs. Outside, from the balcony, the world was cold and colourless in the dawn, the bay below, the further islands beyond, like the black-and-white scenery which had flowed beneath the windows of the flitter the evening before.

He thumbed the big red switch which cut off the zappies and opened the gate through the balcony-rail onto the diving board. For some minutes, he paused on the board, admiring the scene as it slowly flushed and warmed into life. Then, taking a short run, he flung himself out and down into the huge updraft from the wind-deflectors. With arms outspread, he floated slowly down on roaring pillows of air and gently sank into the water, which creamed around him like champagne.

"Deshcripe der egshperience again pliss," said Dr. Gespenster authoritatively. Leaning back behind his desk, he was a bulky figure; his eyes looked out blandly through gold-rimmed pince-nez in the general direction of Paradine; beneath his neatly-pointed beard, his cravat overflowed from an old-fashioned wing collar, and his plump hands were pressed together as if in prayer. He seemed everything that a psychman should be.

Paradine went through it again—the figure in the cabin, the more-than-dream in the sleeping-room.

"So," said the psychman. "So. Der doppelgänger. An old shtory. Ve find him in—vot you call—märchen? legents? Ja." He raised his voice suddenly. "Vy did you identify der figure mit yourself?"

"Well, it was mainly the eyes, doctor. It was like looking at myself in a reversal-mirror."

"Ach, der eyes, der vindow off der soul, der poet says. Shmaltz. Pfui. Haff you any history of brain damache?"

"None."

"Epilepsy?"

"No."

"Ve can eliminate. Der dishturbance is psychic in orichin. You haff anxieties?"

"Yes, I have."

"Business? personal?"

"Both."

"So, now orsodox diagnoses voot tell us—" he paused impressively—"dat der doppelgänger halluc- ination is der projection off an anxiety shtate. If der figure hat been rich, powerful or sreatening, it voot have inticated a projection off der hyperconscious or monitory factor in der psyche. But since it vos poor and, you say, deshperate, it is derefore a concretiza- tion off feelinks off rejection and inadequacy."

Paradine relaxed a little. Anxiety was real, he had known it most of his life, and the truth seemed bearable.

"But von moment. I say der orsodox diagnosis. But dat is not alvays der Gespenster diagnosis. Listen. Let us make a liddle fantasy. Supposink ve liffed in a vorld where, ven makink decision, ve choose not von but bose alternatives. You comprehend?"

"No—not really, doctor. Such a world would surely become too complex to exist?"

"In time, yes. But imachine a vorld in vich time itself bifurcates. It branches. Zen you voot be liffink in several time-lines, each ignorant off der rest."

"I find that more disturbing than any hallucination."

"So. Now imachine a leakage, a short circuit, an induction, shall ve say, between von time-line and der next. Time energy spills over. Images from von time-line appear elsevere. You follow?"

"Only just."

"Den dere is an appearance vich is not dream, not hallucination and not reality?"

Paradine sat silent for a moment, waiting for him to go on. The psychman remained unmoving, his pince-nez gleaming, his beard poised above his judicious hands.

"What are you advising me, doctor? To ignore it? to pretend it isn't there?"

"Treat it," said the psychman, "as an unusual und interestink natural phenomenon. If it recurs, observe, report, be not disturbed. For der nervous abreactions, I vill send you a prescription. For der rest, vork, play, make loff, enchoy yourself. Not to vorry. Ve are vorkink on der problem."

When Paradine had left, the psychman remained for some moments motionless and silent, before directing his voice to the intercom on his desk.

"Immediate," he said in a monotone, "personal. Message to Mrs. Helena Paradine, from Doctor Gespenster. Your husband has agreed to remain under observation at my clinic for the next forty-eight hours.

Please send clothing and personal effects. Message ends."

He remained leaning back in his chair, palms together, beaming benevolently through gold rims. Behind him the front of a tall filing-cabinet clicked and opened all the way down, like a door, revealing a roomy cupboard within. The chair rolled silently backwards on the thick carpet, carrying the smiling doctor, still motionless except for an almost imperceptible raising of the heels. A vac-tube snaked out from the wall and hissed over him, removing any dust. He drew back snugly into the steel cupboard, the door clicked shut, and with a faint humming the temperature and humidity controls took over.

Emerging from the private subway-shuttle, Paradine strolled slowly through the halls and public rooms of Kraagshaven. The psychman had reassured him, and he felt at ease. He had left the office early; there was plenty of time; the late afternoon sun struck in across the terraces and through the high arched windows, illuminating a piece of sculpture, turning a fountain into rainbows, blocking out majestic hallways into gloom and gold. He snapped his fingers, and an autobar trundled up to him and served a perfect martini.

There was complete silence everywhere, except for the sound of fountains and the faintest stir from the air-conditioning. No house-guests, no select dinner party; but as he approached the seaward side, a serving-hatch whispered open, and an autotable set for two wheeled itself silently down the corridor. Curious, he followed it until it came to rest on the small private balcony inlaid with blue tiles, where he dined with Helena on the rare occasions when they were alone. How pleasant, and how kind of Helena, to think—and then, from another balcony high above, he heard her laughter, and a man's answering it.

One of the many private lifts ran up in the giant buttress of the wall. He thumbed the concealed switch and shot silently upwards. The door slid open onto the long oval bedroom.

The faintest sound of the lift must have disturbed Helena, for she was pulling the filmy billows of the thermocloak around her, and seemed flushed and surprised.

"I thought—but the psychman said you were staying on at the clinic. I sent your things."

"No?" He was puzzled. "He said nothing—you don't seem very delighted to see me."

"Of course I'm delighted," she said, suddenly swinging her legs off the bed and walking quickly towards him. "It's just—the surprise, and you came so early." She put her arms around him, and the thin film of the thermocloak seemed like nothing. But her eyes, in enormous close-up, stared at him hard and frightened; and below her perfume lingered another perfume, more elusive, more aggressive, a man's scent. Still staring into her eyes, he deliberately blanked his mind three times; and each time the first picture triggered in his mind by that underscent was the face of Billy Merganser.

Swinging her away from him, he looked quickly around the oval room, glowing now in the dusk as the soft lights came on. No one could hide there. In the tall window, a flicker of shadowy movement caught his eye.

"No," said Helena sharply, and caught grimly at his arm. He pushed her sprawling across the bed, and ran out onto the balcony. The gate in the railing was open, and Billy Merganser stood poised near the far end of the diving board. He was dressed in a loose white jacket and embroidered beachpants, and his hair, puffed out by the roaring updraft, was startling white in contrast to the deep artificial bronze of his skin. He spun around to face Paradine, the smile sick and frozen on his face.

Paradine looked down at the red switch which cut out the zappies.

"Jump," he shouted. "Jump, you pinkeyed buckrabbit. Why don't you jump?"

With a yell of laughter, Merganser spun round and leaped out into the void.

"I'll bifurcate you," screamed Paradine, and his hand swept down and hovered over the red switch.

There was an infinitely fine hesitation; the time-lines divided.

(Paradine ... 1211 slowly withdrew his hand from the switch. Twisting like a cat as he floated down the updraught, Merganser struck the water cleanly and swam towards one of the openings of the lower terrace.

Paradine walked back into the oval bedroom, to find his wife sitting up on the bed, coolly watching him. There was nothing more to be said; a decisive moment had passed. A week later, Bill Merganser was back. As the years went on, he became more and more a permanent guest. The corporation ran KRAS-CO, and Helena exercised the necessary personal direction as well as any man. Paradine spent more and more time at Kraagshaven. When there were guests, he would startle them by hurling champagne-glasses into the updraught, where the zappies turned them into brief streaks of stardust. At other times they would dine together, the three of them, Helena, Merganser and Paradine, by artificial candlelight on some secluded balcony. But more often still, they would not see him for weeks at a time, as he wandered like a nomad through the vast halls and multifarious rooms and secret passageways of Kraagshaven, watching the changing effects of sun, starlight or the binary moons, eating and drinking what the autotrolleys brought him, sleeping wherever he happened to lie down on the deep soft sensuous carpets.)

Paradine ... 1212 knocked down the switch. As Merganser dived desperately, twisting in the howling air, the zappies came on and coughed and coughed again, and his fine clothes and his fine body whirled upwards in a scream and a puff of red mist and a long streak of bloody rags.

There was no answering scream from inside the bedroom. Silent, white-faced and blazing-eyed, Helena already had her hand on the emergency button of the communicator. He pulled it from her hand, tossed it out of the window to the zappies and sprang to the still-open door of the private lift. Reaching with his fingernail under the main panel, he opened a small concealed section of the panelling and thumbed the switch inside it. With a faint rush of air, the lift slipped downwards.

Old man Kraag had told him about this once. There had been times, in the earlier days, when he had had to take certain risks; it was wise to have an escape hatch. Although it had not been needed for many years, Aino had, in his methodical way, kept it all in working order; and Paradine was grimly thankful for this now. Much had been lost; but life could still be pleasant.

The lift shot down, below the lowest terrace, below the service basement. When the panel slid open, he stepped out into a cave deep in the solid rock, full of wet sea-smell and the soft sound of water from the green pool at the end which, gently rising and falling, was the underwater outlet to the bay.

From a niche in the wall he took down a small communicator, brushed away the film of moisture from the dial, and tuned in.

"Aino? Aino?"

A grunt answered.

"Aino—escape emergency—proceed as planned—immediate."

Another grunt. It was enough.

Hanging against the wall was a scuba-suit, dull-green and almost invisible in the water. He quickly checked the airbottles, the infra-red goggles and the underwater sled. The tiny radar-jammer gave him some trouble; it had been affected by the damp, and he had to carry it over to the light of the lift, open and reset it before it began to operate. The hitch unsettled him and, as he stood with all his gear on by the edge of the salt pool, he hesitated for a moment.

A hesitation, a wavering instantaneous stasis, a faint sense of strain in the matrix. Then the time-lines separated.

(Paradine ... 12121 pushed the sled into the pool and dropped in after it. He swam carefully through the tunnel, pushing the sled in front of him, until he

69

came out into open water lit by the fading green glimmer of twilight. Then he activated the compressed-air motor of the sled, gripped the rudder-bar and was drawn swiftly and silently through the water.

Suddenly the water seemed to boil around him, and he remembered too late the curtain of bubbles which, pumped from pipes on the seabed, broke the waves in the mouth of the bay. The powerful uprush of air spun him over and over, losing control of the sled, which skittered away into the darkness. With a rush he broke surface and lay there, floundering helplessly and unable to dive again, in the churning bubbling water.

There was a whicker of rotorblades overhead, and a bright cone of light fastened on him. Smoothly the police flitter swooped down, to pouch him neatly in its scoop-net, and rise again, and carry him away to the landing slip.

The long trial was a legal classic, and resulted in a verdict of fifth degree murder with plea for moderate clemency, five years of corrective restraint and permanent deprivation of civic right. While he was under restraint, Helena obtained a divorce with full property separation, and lived to be very old, very rich and very wicked. Paradine . . . 12121 thus lost control of Helena, KRASCO and Kraagshaven, forever.)

With a sudden catch at the heart, Paradine ... 12122 remembered the bubble curtain. There was a moment of pure panic, until he remembered the other hidden switch in the lift. Thumbing it off, he made swiftly back to the pool.

Drawn by the sled, he slipped silently along beneath the waters of the bay, undetectable to searching police flitters. Once past the mouth of the bay, he followed the shoreline northward for nearly two hours, surfacing briefly to sight landmarks. At last he came to the other cave, which wound up through the cliffs to the old abandoned signal-station, where faithful Aino was waiting with the clothes and the money-pouches and the concealed racing-flitter.

Years later, there was a man who lived in a white seaport-city among the hot countries. The city had contrived to belong to no one country in particular, and thus remained what it always had been, thieves' kitchen, bargain basement, joy-shop, lost men's paradise.

He was known simply as Master Seth, and he was a most respected citizen. All day long he would sit in his long cool office in the square near the heliport. Although old Aino kept him in splendid physical condition, he had put on weight; only his eyes, in his massive dark face, remained young and lean as he watched continually the movement of the clerks (many of them his own children) at the counters, and the swarms of tourists, who came in their innocence to change their money and be mildly but methodically gypped before they set out again lusting for bargains.

Favourite customers were always welcome to chat with him at his desk. He would offer them iced rum-coffee, and charm them with his old-fashioned courtesy, while his young eyes flickered discreetly over them and about the busy chattering room, and his long plump fingers played with the stacks of notes on his desk and the rouleaux of coins—bright beadels, tiny sprugs, semi-deniers, golden fands, muldoons, zaks, grisbs—in their wooden trays. He was almost a tourist attraction himself; they would say " ... and of course you must change your money at Master Seth's; he'll skin you a little, in a perfectly charming way, but it's worth it—he can tell you all the best places to spend it."

In the late evenings, he would sit at his usual table in a quiet café by the seafront, where the palm trees clattered their stiff fronds in the night-breeze, and the binary moons wove their changing pattern of light across the water. Beside him would be dishes of shelled prawns and baby squid, anchovies and black olives and bread rolls, from which he would eat delicately with his plump fingers. He would drink chilled fish-wine, and play double-checkers with the chief of customs or the harbourmaster, and the policeman on

71

the beat would salute respectfully when he caught his eye.

Later he would walk home through the magnolia-scented night, with faithful Aino padding barefoot behind him along the dusty road, to the huge rambling white house on the edge of the town. There was always someone to welcome him home, for he kept three wives there, and several girls. He had raised his various families harmoniously together, though he had given up trying to keep count of them; there were strange young faces in the house now, and new babies tumbling about the wide verandahs who, he supposed, were grandchildren.

Often, as his eyes flickered about the counting-house, or as he sat over the game of double-checkers, or as he walked home by the light of the binary moons, he would think back with satisfaction on his long life. So many problems to consider; so many decisions to take; so many things that might have gone wrong. He sighed with satisfaction; he had made the right decisions after all, life might have been a great deal worse.

His children grew up, and his grandchildren, and his greatgrandchildren. The diverging time-lines passed on into the endlessly meshing polydimensional fans of a myriad subuniverses. Many of Master Seth's descendants were quite commonplace, almost monolinear. Not all were honest; some died young. One had a superb voice, and travelled the world, singing. One became a soldier of fortune, and won immortal glory at the Battle of the Nine Rivers. One was, quite unjustly, shot for cowardice. Several others came to violent ends, one in a quarrel over cards, three lost at sea, one drowned through falling, drunk, into a vat of fish-wine.

One went away, and discovered and marketed the elixir of everlasting life. This resulted in a slow but cumulative overload on an infinite number of time-paths. The overload built up until it flashed over and fed back at time-speed along all the convergent subuniverses, blowing out one time-line after another.

The time-nodes fused or shorted out in soundless millennial arcs of chronokinetic energy; doppelgängers ran screaming and wild-eyed through all the familiar streets. The entire matrix collapsed, became rigidly monolinear.

FIVE

"He calls it the Initiation Room," said the girl in the grey dress. "I wonder why? It sounds kinky, doesn't it?"

The long gallery, which at first sight appeared straight, was in fact so curved and lit that the end was out of sight. It was an uncomfortable place, which forced the visitor to go on without knowing where, and this, Paradine knew, was deliberate. He felt rather the same way about the girl whom he had met at the door. She was wearing what they called the Pure Look, a plain grey dress, rather short, sleeveless, small white collar; bare feet; no visible makeup; hair bleached white; and an enormously exaggerated pair of horn-rimmed glasses. She looked like a nasty knowing child.

"It's one of his little jokes," said Paradine. "You see?"

He pointed to the row of full-size copies of famous paintings along the invisibly curving wall, all painstakingly disfigured; the Mona Lisa with a property beard, the Birth of Venus scribbled over with children's drawings of ships and airplanes, Whistler's Mother smoking a corncob pipe.

"How blah," she said, "oldy, gagaist stuff. He must be retrogressing."

"It's the beginning," said Paradine. "Let's keep going—it gets worse—or better."

Madame Recamier reclining in black lace underwear. Millet's Gleaners as a cornflake advertisement. Goya's Firing Squad with the word KERBLAM coming out of each musket in a little balloon.

"Fun," said the girl flatly. "Horrid dreary fun."

"Keep going," said Paradine.

They walked on down the curving corridor, until they came to Cézanne's Apples, dry and shrivelled, on a cloth stained by their own decay; and Manet's

Barmaid at the Folies Bergères, the freshness gone, a flabby woman with a knowing smile; and the Rembrandt self-portrait, unchanged, until you noticed the smell, sprayed from concealed atomisers in the frames. The smell of rotten apples, of cheap scent and cheap cigars, of an old unwashed body in a closed dirty room.

The girl stared at the Rembrandt, her surprise magnified by the enormous trick-lenses; then she gagged. Suddenly liking her a little, Paradine laughed and pulled her away.

"You've got the message," he said. "It's not really a joke. It says art's like that and life's like that."

"Well aren't they?" she said, recovering herself, and he ceased to like her. "Aren't they? I just don't want to know, is all. How bloody blah it all is. I want a drink."

"And you shall have one, sweetie," said Hyperion Merganser's soft voice. "Come in, you're initiated now. Dr. Paradine, how pleasant." He was standing in the doorway, set at an angle so that they could only glimpse the glowing room beyond. He too was wearing the fashionable plain grey suit, like the other men and women who were now drifting towards the door; and Paradine wondered whether the vogue for bleached hair and exaggerated lenses was a public tribute to Merganser's albinism.

He went before them with his swaying walk towards the centre of the room, and concealed lighting in the overhead panels sprang to life. The guests were transformed, and Paradine could no longer recognise the girl he had met in the hall, for like the others, like himself, she became part of the shifting pattern of shapes and colours. The plain grey suits and dresses fluoresced into deep bright lines, or shifted and rippled, or glowed into calligraphic designs, or, under certain lights, became no more than a ghostly transparency. The white hair glowed blue or golden, or glittered, or shimmered.

Paradine spoke to the girl, or one exactly like her, who now had midnight-blue hair powdered with stars, and whose dress was an opalescent mist. A face

75

suddenly appeared beside them offering drinks on a tray; the servant, dressed in close-fitting matt-black, was invisible in the strange lights except for a white face with malicious eyes and a whispering mouth. The drink seemed to float into his hand; swallowed, it was almost tasteless but produced euphoria.

Presently they sauntered over to the middle of the room, where something lay on a block of green marble.

"What is it?" said the girl.

"It's the last of Fioredespina's tactiles," said Paradine, "some say it was the old man's greatest. Close your eyes; touch it; run your hands over it."

The girl did so, and he watched the sudden play of interest and pleasure in her face, before closing his eyes and permitting himself to touch the surface, running his fingertips over it at first. It felt as fresh and gay as it had been on the day when the master first carved and imprinted it. He let his fingers wander swiftly over it, sampling its variety, feeling the surfaces shift faintly as they adjusted to his personality, sensing the light warmth of the girl's personality here and there, lingering above the dry dark wisdom of the master impressed into the whole. He let the girl's personality mingle pleasantly with his own for a while, before choosing a place where he might meditate with his whole palm resting on a deeper and more enigmatic passage. Immediately he had a sense of laughter that was pure and wise at first, but rapidly became overlaid, ran up the scale, became an epicene giggle.

He jerked his eyelids open, and saw Merganser's hand beside his, Merganser's face grinning slyly into his own. He roughly withdrew his hand, and the tactile seemed to go dead as he did so.

"What the hell have you got this here for?" he said.

"Perhaps because I've got to have something in this place that isn't fake," murmured Merganser. "Or perhaps not. Now hush—you'll miss our speaker."

He glided over to the centre of the room, and the lights over him contracted into a spot, in which his fluff of albinoid hair shone like an improper halo.

76

"Boys and girls," he said in a voice that carried through the chatter, "I would like you all to meet our guest speaker, Professor Leonardo Quist. He has come to tell us of a great thing, nothing less than the death of art, and its renewal. Professor Quist."

He retired from the ring of light, drawing into it as he did so a very short dark broad man with a spade beard and a shock of dark hair which seemed to give out sparks as he ran his hand across it.

"*Not* ladies and gentlemen," he said. "People. You listening. I proclaim the death of art. It's no secret. It's dead. The art galleries—catacombs, cemeteries, middens." He munched out his words angrily, as if he hated them and despised his audience. The crowd shifted agreeably towards him.

"Some of you maybe didn't know that. So we played a trick on you. A cheap trick. You got the point. All the art we know is a cheap trick. It strikes noble attitudes. It pretends to discover things about the world. It's a lie. It leaves out all the real things, the sweat and bellyache and obscenity."

Paradine was quietly edging his way out to the back of the crowds and along the far wall, near the concealed service entrances. All the time he could hear the little bearded man munching and spitting out his words.

"The artist believes his own lie. It's makes him important. He preaches that art is contingent, that it depends on the will of a maker. He even invents a god who makes things. Then he says, Look, I'm like god, I also make things. Worship me. But everything he makes is fake. It's false, rotten, dead, It's buried in cemeteries called art galleries. There's only one thing to do with a cemetery. Drive a bulldozer through it."

Slipping behind one of the wall screens, Paradine unzipped his suit and stuffed it down a disposal-chute. Underneath, he wore the same matt-black skin-tight suit as the servants, and a cap drawn over his head concealed all except his eyes.

"Art, like life, is governed by necessity," snarled Quist. "Cause and effect. No contingency, no making. A world of necessary reactions. I show you the begin-

nings of a new art. It is the only art, the art of
necessity. Come. Look."

As he led the crowd towards the tall grey rectangle
that seemed to hang in mid-air near the other wall,
Paradine waited patiently for the moment when all
eyes would be fixed on the demonstration.

Quist tapped the grey sheet, and it rang softly. "A
passive, sensitive medium," he said. "Like the human
mind. Sensitive to weather, time, seasons, the daily
statistical averages. Sensitive to you. Sensitive to me.
Heartbeat, body temperature, metabolic rhythms, al-
pha-waves, secretion levels. All with positive feed-
back. The art of necessity. See."

He reached out his right forefinger. The grey sheet
came to life, a rigid geometrical pattern wove itself
out, split, and began to bleed streams of coloured
dross.

Paradine moved at once. Lifting the wafer-thin dial
of his watch, he revealed underneath it another dial
that glowed with tiny phosphorescent dots. Turning
swiftly about, he waited until all the dots coincided at
one side of the dial, then walked unerringly over to
the wall at that point. Face to the wall, in his black
suit, he was invisible. He dropped his arms to his
sides, slowed his pulse and breathing, mounted with
practised ease to the seventh degree of concentration,
and remained rigid, only subliminally aware of his
surroundings, while his personal time-clock ticked off
three hours in his mind.

When he moved again, the room was velvet-dark,
and the luminous dots in his wrist-detector still pointed unerringly to the wall in front of him. With precise
movements, he removed from a pouch the three small
domed objects and pressed them one by one against
the wall, to which they adhered with a click. He
looked at the wrist-detector; the glowing dots had
gone out; all the alarm-systems—infra-red, radar,
body-heat, pressure-sensitive—would remain blanked
out for a period of fifteen minutes. Using a small
glow-torch, he stepped to the centre of the room and
picked up the tactile. It was surprisingly light, and as
his fingers brushed the modulated surface he felt the

78

dry ironical laughter, before slipping it into the carrier-bag.

As he glided between the sliding doors into the hallway and extinguished the glow-torch, he knew that he was virtually safe. It was only his trained unsleeping senses that picked up the faint silent movement of air in the darkness. He wove aside in a defensive crouch, but hampered by the carrier-bag on his back, he was a fraction slow. The blow descended on his right arm, paralysing it, filling him with pain and nausea.

With trained precision, he imposed on himself the third degree of concentration, which enables the adept to control pain. Something big in the darkness; his foot went up in a savate-kick to the knee. There was a sharp click and a hiss of pain. As the attacker stumbled forward, Paradine stiffened his left arm and struck upwards with the deadly blow to the heart. He was still able to catch the big body and lower it with a soft padded thud to the floor.

The lights came on. Rembrandt on his panel shot up with a click, and out of the opening came two black-clad guards, each cradling the stubby barrel of a nerve-gun. Behind and between them, white hair like a halo, pink eyes shining with mockery, walked Merganser.

"Keep quite still, Doctor Paradine," he said. "One of these guns can burn out every motor-nerve in your body and leave you paralysed for life."

He watched while the guards searched Paradine, and removed the concealed knife and the tiny stun-gun, as well as the Fioredespina tactile in its carrier, and stood him against the wall.

"I'm surprised he managed to wing you," said Merganser, nodding at Paradine's hanging right arm. He knelt and dragged the black hood off the dead man, revealing a bald head and thick ugly broken features.

"A cheap hoodlum," he said. "His name's Kraag. He doesn't matter, of course, except for one thing." He looked up at Paradine. "This makes it robbery with murder. You'll get the full treatment for that, won't you? They'll send you to the Rehabilitation Centre, and you'll come out of it with half a brain."

He stood up, dusting his knees, and walked slowly towards the opening where the old body-smelling Rembrandt had been.

"You're rather out of luck, aren't you, Doctor Paradine?" he said over his shoulder. "You can take a risk now and wind up a hopeless paralytic, or you can stand trial and spend the rest of your life as a mindless idiot. Perhaps we should have a little talk about it."

One of the guards prodded Paradine in the back with the nozzle of the nerve-gun, and they followed Merganser down the corridor into a hidden room. It was bare, white, plain, with a communications panel along one wall and a bare desk. Merganser seated himself behind it, and motioned Paradine to a chair. One guard stood behind him; the other went out silently through a further door.

"We've been watching you for some time," said Merganser. "Doctor Paradine, the world's finest art thief. We've admired your methods. These delousing devices of yours"—he picked up one of the little dome-shaped objects from the table—"they're really good. Better than anything we've got."

Paradine nodded ironically. "I'd like to know one thing, if you don't mind. Where did I come unstuck?"

Merganser's smile broadened as he picked up the carrier and drew out Fioredespina's tactile.

"The only detector that really matters," he said, "is in here, where else? ... You're an art-historian, Paradine, what made you an art-thief? Better pay?"

"That," said Paradine, "and ... I was sick of seeing beautiful things in the hands of fools."

"A worthy motive," said the albino, and sat looking at him, as if waiting for him to speak.

"Well," said Paradine impatiently, "what are we waiting for? Haven't you called the police?"

"Not so fast, dear boy. There is another possibility. Have you heard of the Troublemaker?"

"A person?" said Paradine.

"No, a thing. Not a very large thing. We have one

piece of information about it. It operates on some principle which is directly opposed to all the known laws of Nature. If it is ever switched on, the results would be, quite literally, beyond comprehension."

"Where is it?" said Paradine.

"They've got it," said Merganser. "We know exactly where. We want it—to keep it out of the wrong hands, of course."

"Of course," said Paradine. "And you want me to get it, I suppose. What's the deal?"

Merganser leaned forward. "We'll see you into the country," he said. "Once you're there, your only way out will be by the proper escape-route—with the Troublemaker, of course. If and when you get back here, we'll forget about the little accident. And as a bonus, we'll give you—this." He brushed his fingers lightly over the tactile. "It's logical isn't it?"

"When do I start?" said Paradine.

"As soon as we've fixed your arm and given you your orders. There's only one really. In case of trouble, find Alexander the Great, and do what he tells you."

The other guard returned to the room with cups of thick Turkish coffee and little glasses of ice-water.

"It's quite safe to drink," said Merganser. "I'm not playing any more tricks—for the present."

The submarine surfaced about a mile off shore and lay with its decks awash, moving uncomfortably in the troughs of the long slow rollers. Climbing out of the hatch into the dazzle of the early morning sun, Paradine caught a glimpse of the low hazy shoreline, and of the shape of mountains far inland. There was not time to look: the captain was anxious to submerge and get away. The crew had been under orders to speak to him as little as possible; there was a brief impersonal handshake from the captain and good wishes for whatever he was doing. Then two crewmen helped him over the side with his surfboard, and he paddled away, while the submarine disappeared in a slick of bubbles. He was alone, a mile off shore, dressed only in briefs and goggles, his body deeply bronzed with artificial tan, paddling the board and waiting for a big one.

Presently it came in behind him, a massive ridge of water that lifted him and rolled him in towards the distant shore. He drew himself up and balanced on the board, which rode down perpetually along the gleaming slope of blue water marbled with white foam. The hill of water towered higher and higher behind him, and the off-shore breeze slashed and hurled the tops of it away in flying spindrift. The stealthy silent movement of the great mass quickened and broke into a hissing roar, and the great wave leaned up and over into the wind and curved over him in a cascading tunnel of green glass, and broke again, and he came through, breathless from under the tons of water, and slid in the broken shallows up towards the beach.

A young man was waiting for him by the edge of the sea, a trim tanned young man with sun-bleached fair hair cut close to the skull and blue eyes that seemed faded by the sun.

"Like a bird," he said, "you came in like a bird. Where are you from?"

"From following the sun around," said Paradine, "like the birds."

The young man drew a pattern of straight lines with his toe in the wet sand and Paradine turned the tall surfboard so as to show the other side, with the same design in broad lines of red. The water rippled in and washed out the lines in the sand.

The young man flashed his white teeth. "I'm Vince," he said.

"I'm Seth. Glad to know you."

"Come up the beach. I've got a set of wheels there. Let's go and get some breakfast."

Beyond the sandhills was Vince's open runabout; they slid the surfboard onto the rack, and drove off down a rough country road.

"We'll probably keep you a couple of days," said Vince, "then we'll move off slowly towards the high country. We'll work our way along at odd jobs till we get to the mountains. Then a couple of the boys will see you across. No need to move too far or too fast, it might attract attention. But we can't leave it too long either, it'll soon be getting a bit late in the season for the high passes."

"I still don't get it," said Paradine. "Why all the secrecy? We're safe enough here, aren't we?" He looked out at the simple but well-ordered country-side, the green paddocks, the sparse white farm-houses nestled behind their windbreaks.

"Safe enough," said Vince, with his blue eyes stead-ily on the road, "as long as you understand the set-up. This is a nice country, no great social problems, no great social evils. We like to keep it that way, so we're rather careful about the kind of people and the kind of ideas we let in. We don't want anyone too clever, or too rich, or too enthusiastic about anything. We haven't much power and we don't want it. So we like to be friendly with everyone in a cool sort of way."

"You mean that what I'm doing might seem un-friendly to someone?"

"I don't know what you're doing," said Vince, lifting his blue eyes briefly from the road and glancing at Paradine, "except just following the sun around. If you want to have a look at the high country while you're here, that's jake with me."

They passed a country school, with the fat bare-footed children marching in from morning roll-call.

"I like it here," said Paradine.

"It's not a bad sort of place," said Vince indifferently.

Vince's place was up in the hills outside the city, a small house surrounded by bush, but set upon piles so that by day one could look down on the long reach of the harbour, the clusters of low red-roofed buildings, and the dark angular shapes of the wharves. At night, the lines of the harbour and the town were picked out in rows of blue and orange road-lamps, and there was a reflected glare of working-lights from the ship-ping at the wharves.

The bush hushed in the night breeze; the bright stars wheeled on their regular way; triggered by the warm night air, a late cicada trilled its automatic locator signal.

Vince poured himself another beer, and perched on the verandah-rail. Paradine leaned back in the chair.

"I like it here," he said again.

"It's not bad," said Vince. "A bit slow."

"That's why I like it. It's like the rest of the world fifty years ago. You've got a different kind of time here."

"We've got a utopia here," said Vince, "and in utopia, time stops, inevitably. The end of an evolutionary chain, perfect adaptation, perfect stability."

"Degeneration?"

"Doesn't follow. Listen—there's a bird we've got— there might be one out there in the bush, but they're pretty rare. It's a dumpy bird"—he made a shape with his hands—"and it's forgotten how to fly, but it's sort of dull-coloured and minds its own business and doesn't flap around or make a noise. It just stays that way. There's no reason it should ever die out—"

Out in the bush, a point of red light winked; there was a sound like a slap. Vince tumbled forward off the verandah-rail, and his glass fell and smashed. At the same time, Paradine dived sideways off the low chair and slithered across the floor towards him. There was the abrupt roar of a motorcycle starting down the hill.

Vince was lying on his face, and there was a small dark hole in his back with a dark seepage around it; but when Paradine turned him over and lifted his head, the blood was already welling in his throat. He choked and dribbled on it, staring up at Paradine with wondering blue eyes.

"Get out—we're blown," he said laboriously. "Try Merv—Merv—he's expensive—but good—Merv—bar nothing."

He began to choke again, and when it was over Paradine laid him down and left him, the faded blue eyes still staring. He had liked Vince, but there was no point in leaving any clues. He washed carefully and exchanged his bloodstained shirt and denims for some that had belonged to the dead man, and added a thick pullover. There were three crowns in Vince's wallet, and no other money in the house.

He thought about the car, and decided it would be safer to use it and ditch it as soon as possible. The surfboard had already been disposed of, but the equipment which had been carried in the compartment inside it was now stowed in an old dufflebag. He looked around carefully to make sure he had left no traces, hefted the bag and went out, closing the door.

Threading his way through the early morning crowds, Paradine moved up the main street, dufflebag slung over his shoulder, like any other drifting young man looking for a job or a ship or a hitch or a friend to drink with. The crowd piled up around an intersection, waiting for the lights to turn. He had to find a man named Merv in a city of half a million people; there was no use in looking for that one in the phone book. "Merv—bar nothing"—nickname? His eyes moved restlessly, abstractedly taking in the details of the unfamiliar street, and the signs: Men's Fashions ... Tie Bar ... Numodes ... Perfume Bar ... Central Hotel ... Public Bar ... Private Bar ... Bar BQ ...

Bar Nothing; there was something that he could look up in the phonebooth on the corner. He found it, and the sidestreet in which it stood, a sleazy coffee bar with a red neon sign, Bar NOthing, which flashed on and off, but always leaving the fiery O in place.

Inside, there were small tables and chairs with spindly black-iron legs and shaded lights and a sandwich counter. A solitary girl was sitting at one of the tables, staring down into her coffee-cup. He bought himself a black coffee and a sandwich and sat down silently opposite her. The girl looked up; she was tall and thin, with a dark serious face and long hair.

"I'm looking for Merv," he said.

"I'm hungry," she said in a low voice. "Buy me another coffee and a sandwich and we'll talk."

He brought the coffee and sandwich, and she said: "How much money have you got?"

"Two crowns," he said.

85

She sighed. "There's a machine over there. It costs you a crown to play. There's a big jackpot in it, it's been building up for days. Maybe you can hit it."

"Show me," he said.

She stood up and walked over to the machine, a tall thin girl dressed in a sweat-shirt and old blue jeans. The machine had a dial like a video set, where coloured dots of light swam about in a rapid random pattern. Underneath were three plastic keys coloured red, yellow and blue to match the dots. There was a coin-slot at the side, and below it a wide metal hopper that promised ample wealth.

"How do you play?" he said.

"Each key fixes one dot," she said, waving a hand vaguely. "You have to get the three dots in an equithingally triangle. Then the band plays."

"Let's have a try," he said, putting a crown in the slot. He would have to play it this once to get the feel of it, then make the real try. He leaned forward, sliding his fingers down the sides of the machine, feeling for a vibration, and found it, low down on the left side. The red key clicked down, and one red dot fixed itself near the centre of the screen. Now the yellow, not too far away. Now the blue, and the three points of light shone out, forming a long skew triangle. He rested his left hand lightly on the machine; the vibration had stopped.

The girl sighed again, and turned away.

Paradine pushed his last crown into the slot, and all the dots came on, swirling about in their haphazard pattern. They must be controlled from a simple randomizer whose vibrations he had sensed on the left side of the machine. If it were shorted out, the pattern would stabilize itself. He slipped from his pocket one of the small domed objects he had used in the raid on Bill Merganser's gallery, and held it lightly against the side of the machine. Three dots steadied in the centre of the screen, and blazed white. A taped brass-band struck up "Happy Days Are Here Again" and a mass of coins crashed down into the hopper and spilled over onto the floor.

The girl was down on her knees beside him, help-

ing him to shovel them up and drop them into the
duffle-bag.

"You made it," she said happily. "Gee, you're lucky.
Last-chancers never make it, but you made it."

She held up the last crown in her long thin fingers.
"Buy me another coffee and a sandwich," she said.
"Then I'll take you to see Merv."

Merv's place was an old unpainted wooden bun-
galow up a steep side-street, behind a new factory.
The garden was a tangle of tall grass and shrubs run
wild; the tall wooden piles and the rickety wooden
stairway that ran up to the front verandah were
matted over with creepers. On the verandah were
many cases of empty quart beer-bottles, and the door
stood open.

Inside, a bearded man was lying asleep, sprawling
on his back, fully-dressed, on the big iron bed. The
girl touched him lightly on the hand and said: "Merv,
wake up, It's me."

The bearded man sat up, instantly alert, and
swung his legs over the edge of the bed.

"G'day, Sue," he said. "You oughter bin here last
night. Gee, we had a beaut booze-up. All the gang
was here. You oughter bin here."

"I was working," the girl said shortly. "I brought
someone to see you. His name's Seth."

Merv looked Paradine up and down; behind the
fluffy beard, his face was lean and foxy, and his
close-set eyes were only slightly bloodshot.

"I need help," said Paradine. "Vince sent me."

"Vince is dead, mate," said Merv.

"I know. I was there when it happened. That's why
I'm here."

The girl kicked under the edge of the bed, and
three more empty bottles rolled out. "You might have
saved us a drop," she said sulkily.

"There's a coupler riggers stowed away behind the
bath. Get them out, will you? and fix me a feed while
you're about it. I'll have the chops from the fridge
and a coupler eggs."

87

The girl shrugged and strolled off towards the back of the house.

"Now what's the proposition, mate?" said Merv.

"I want to go east and cross the mountains."

"Why?"

"That's my business."

"Suit yourself, mate. How much you got?"

Paradine tipped the money out on the table. "879 crowns, 16 coronets and a bauble," he said.

Merv pulled an old suit-case from under the bed and swept all the money into it. "She'll do, mate," he said. "Hey, Sue, put on the sausages and fry up a couple more eggs."

After breakfast they sat and smoked on the verandah, half-hidden by a matted curtain of creeper. Merv was carefully cleaning a rifle with a piece of oily rag.

"There's no time to take it slow and make it look convincing," he said. "I want to get rid of you quick as I can. So we'll take the old truck and head straight up country. Scout around for a few days and maybe shoot a pig or two. When it's all clear, we'll go up one of the bush tracks and into the high country. There's a road over the pass, but it's closed at the border anyway, so we'll go on foot. I'll see you over to the other side, but I stop at the snow-line. Okay?"

"Suits me," said Paradine. "It's the sooner the better as far as I'm concerned."

"That all your stuff?" said Merv, nodding towards the duffle bag. "What's in it?"

"Just some things I need."

"Suit yourself, mate. Hey, Sue," he called. The girl came out from washing the breakfast dishes and looked at him indifferently. "Mind the shop while I'm away, will you?" He patted her on the bottom. "Be a good girl and we'll have a party when I come back. C'mon, Seth, let's get moving."

They hid the truck in the foothills and tramped on, each carrying a swag of food and a blanket, with Merv carrying a rifle and Paradine the duffle bag as well. Merv led the way up a track that grew steeper and rougher as it wound away from the road, up the shoulder of the pass.

Early on the third day, they scrambled cautiously around a high outcrop, and Paradine found himself looking down into the floor of the pass far below. The winding ribbon of road was cut by a dark line of rusted concertina-wire, and there was a concrete pill-box built in against the cliff, and two sentries in drab green uniforms pacing to and fro outside. Nothing else moved in the bleak light. Already there were streaks of early snow lodged among the rocks.

"Used to be a lotter big stone statues down there," said Merv. "They had hollow heads. When the wind blew, you could hear them way down the pass, singing like choirboys. Give you the creeps. Had to shift 'em when the road went through. Put 'em in the museum. They don't sing there anymore."

A bitter wind was blowing up the pass, and dark masses of cloud were building up beyond the ridges. "Let's get going," said Merv. "There's snow on the way."

The descent took them away from the road, down across scree and scrub, with flurries of snow blowing in their faces. At last they scrambled across a ridge and came out unexpectedly above a stream that dashed down brokenly between high banks towards a wider valley below. Merv pointed down at the narrow shoreline of stones and driftwood that ran along the side of the stream.

"We can follow that down to open country," he said. "It's not as bad as it looks. At least we won't get our feet wet. Hold on while I fix the rope."

Merv turned away, leaving Paradine looking down the valley blurred with snow-gusts. Suddenly the butt of Merv's rifle caught him behind the knees, and at the same time the dufflebag was snatched from his hand. He pitched forward down the steep slope, twisted as he fell, and landed on his feet at the bottom; but at his first step he tripped on a knot of driftwood and went sprawling. There was a soft thud as his swag bounced on the stones beside him. Merv's foxy bearded face peered down at him over the edge of the high bank.

"This is as far as I go, mate," he said, and hefted the dufflebag. "I'll relieve you of this, you've got enough to carry without it. And don't get any ideas, mate. So long." He raised the rifle in threat and salute, and disappeared.

Paradine stared up at the empty skyline, controlling his useless rage. With the dufflebag went his two weapons, the stunner and the pelletgun, all the food-concentrates, the climbing-gear and the night-suit. He reassuringly touched the body-belt in which he carried the three domed interference-devices: those at least were safe. He could not reach the top again without looking lower down for a break in the bank; and even if he did, Merv would be gone, with weapons and knowledge of the ground in his favour. Paradine stood still and breathed slowly, eliminating the last of the energy-consuming rage and effecting control of body-temperature. When he was ready, he shouldered his swag and began to pick his way sure-footedly among the stones, amid flurrying snow; he would need shelter before nightfall.

The provincial town where Paradine was to make his first contact was a dim sprawling derelict place. Once a busy transport centre, it had been damaged in the war and never quite rebuilt, cut off and left to rot when the frontier was sealed off. The market-square was filled with roaring wind and sleet, except where a few forlorn street-lamps made grubby smears of light. An empty street-car clattered slowly past, its pole striking blue flashes from the wire. There was no one about, and no cars; a few dim lights showed in windows. Frozen and half-blinded, Paradine worked his way from doorway to doorway along two sides of the square, dodging between the sleet-squalls, until he came to the square of brown dirty light on the other corner. It was the café, as he expected. Peering through a chink in the blind, he could see a solitary customer sitting there, an old barman dozing beside the steaming urn, a thin array of bottles.

He went in and ordered a coffee and plum-brandy from the old man, and sat down at the table next to the solitary customer. The old-fashioned radio was on, loud enough, with a harsh-voiced announcer reading out agricultural statistics.

Turning his head towards the other man, Paradine murmured: "The winter is early this year."

"They say the snow has never been earlier or deeper in the mountains," said the other.

"Even the seasons have become confused."

"In the time of confusion, violence will reign."

"Will you join me in a drink?" said Paradine.

"With pleasure. We mustn't make it too obvious, but I suggest we move as soon as possible." The other was a pallid, thickset man with bad teeth; he smelt a little.

They sat and drank the bitter coffee and the harsh brandy, talking as two chance-met strangers might, of weather, crops and prices. The radio began to blare out a new patriotic song entitled "We Must All Fight On To Increase The National Potato Yield." The old barman had put on steel-rimmed spectacles and seemed to be dozing over a ragged news-sheet.

When they left, the sleet had ceased and a thin moon was coming out, but the wind, dropping, was still bitter. Paradine felt thankful for the warmth of the cheap brandy as he turned up his collar and splashed along through the black slush on the broken pavement.

"I'm taking you to a temporary place," said his companion. "Luckily it's not far. There's no actual curfew, you understand, but the police don't like night-strollers very much."

"It can't be too short for me," said Paradine. "I've been in the open for over a week."

The other grunted, and said no more.

As they turned out of the main square, a street-car clattered up behind them, and he caught the reflection of its head-light in a window across the street. It picked up their two dark figures in momentary silhouette, and also a third, moving purposefully not far behind them. A chill tension came over him, and he quickened the pace. Fifty yards down the street, a blast of wind came full at them, and he used it to turn his head aside and glance back. The follower came into sight under the corner street-lamp, and was swallowed again in the darkness.

It was time to double-check, hoping that the cover-code was not blown too.

"By the way," he said conversationally, "do you like artichokes?"

The answer should have been: "Yes, but they give my wife indigestion." Instead the man turned his pallid face and bad teeth at him suspiciously, and said: "What's that?"

"Nothing," said Paradine, "just making conversation."

The man grunted, and walked on. He could only be a policeman or a police-agent; there was at least one other behind him; and no doubt it was their job to lead him to the place of capture, perhaps the police-station itself. There was very little time left.

He was now readied for action, breathing deeply and evenly, light on his feet, all senses alert. As they swung round the next corner, he saw with relief that they were in a street of old good houses, the kind that had a deep arched front-doorway as shelter from the weather. Without warning he struck up for the jugular, and the man choked once and fell. In a single movement, Paradine caught him and heaved him into the nearest doorway, where he flattened himself against the brickwork.

The follower's steps came round the corner; his dim shadow passed the archway and went on. Quite silently, Paradine stepped out and went back round the corner, the footsteps already slowing and faltering as he did so.

He had passed only one block when the whistle began to sound; it was answered by others not far away. They seemed to be on all sides of him, but he flung himself desperately into the darkest of the side-streets, hoping that it was not a blind alley.

Strangely, a thin but cheerful music came to him in snatches on the wind. As he ran on, the street opened out on one side, perhaps blasted by bombing in the war. The rubble gave way to waste land, across which, not far away, he could see a few strings of coloured lights, and hear the wheezy music of a steam organ. Some little travelling fair had put up there, perhaps trying to pick up some last few customers before closing down for the winter. Certainly there were not many people about among the wind-blown canvas stalls, but it might be better to take a chance among them than skulk in the rubble with the certainty of being picked up.

He made for the centre of the fair, where the people seemed to be thicker. And there, standing apart from the fat lady, the living skeleton and the fire-eater, was a tent with the sign, in faded gilt lettering, ALEXANDER THE GREAT. He paid his coppers and went in.

The audience, in their rough dark clothes, were bunched close together for warmth on the wooden benches. There was a friendly smell of acetylene, sawdust, sweat, sour beer and fried potatoes. He huddled down in the dark at the end of one of the benches, and waited for the next move.

The Great Alexander was a stout pale man in a shiny old dinner-suit, wearing an opera cloak several sizes too large for him and an opera-hat several sizes too small and a pair of grubby white gloves, and with a large drooping moustache which did not seem to belong to him either. He seemed to Paradine to be the last seedy travesty of all the stage magicians he had ever seen.

"—and now, ladies and gentlemen, may I ask your closest attention for my last little illusion—may I say, the most baffling, hair-raising and death-defying feat of necromancy ever presented on any stage, whose inner secret is known only to myself and a few other initiates. I call it—the Mystery of the Burning Coffin."

As his voice sank to a stage whisper, Paradine

could see the conjurer's eyes flickering restlessly over the crowd, touching him, moving away.

A trolley was wheeled on and carefully placed in the centre of the stage.

"You see," said Alexander, vaguely waving his stick, "there is nothing underneath, and no trap doors."

The fogged and spotty mirrors which were supposed to conceal the drop beneath the trolley were obvious to everyone, but the audience were uncritical. If the magician said it was so, let it be so. A large sheet of stiff paper was laid across the trolley, and an extraordinarily beautiful girl stepped on to the stage.

"Now, my assistant, Miss Helena, will take her place in the coffin."

The magician whispered to her, and her blank blue eyes turned for a second on Paradine. Then she lay down on the trolley and the magician folded up the sides of the paper and taped them to make a box about her, and folded another sheet over the top and taped it down. Colourless fluid was sprinkled over the paper.

"Now—we consign—" he suddenly produced a lighted match "—our beautiful friend—to the flames."

The paper coffin went up in a whoof of blue flame and flakes of black ash, leaving the trolley bare. There was a splatter of applause, which grew louder as Miss Helena came running in from the back of the tent, breathless, with a fixed smile.

"Ladies and gentlemen, thank you for your generous applause. To express our appreciation, and to demonstrate that this astounding illusion does not depend on mere trickery, I should like to try it once more, with a member of the audience. You, sir, at the side there, you look as if you would burn nicely, would you step up please?"

With sudden authority he pointed straight at Paradine, who half rose, and hesitated. The girl Helena was beside him, her fingers gripping his arm with unexpected power. She leaned over, as if helping him, with the same fixed smile and whispered tensely: "It's Alexander—you must do exactly what he says."

He walked stiffly up beside the girl, feeling her warmth and nearness, aware of her perfume, which was not that of a cheap fairground. Then he was on the stage, painfully exposed in the harsh acetylene glare, looking out over the audience, seeing the two burly men in raincoats, who waited inside the door.

He lay down on the trolley: the paper was taped up around him to form a box. Alexander's hands trembled as he worked, and there were beads of sweat on the plump pale face. He bent forward as if examining the paper box and whispered:

"Lie quite still, when you drop through the trap, you'll be under the stage. Back out quietly, do what you're told, and wait for me."

As soon as the paper lid was on and doused with the fluid, Paradine felt the trap give way beneath him. As the paper coffin flashed into flame, he dropped down onto a musty-smelling mattress under the stage, rolled over and over, and found himself in a dimly-lit backstage booth. The blonde girl was helping him up and saying: "Give me your hat and coat. Quickly. Don't you understand? I'm taking your place."

"You'll be caught," said Paradine, stripping off his coat.

"I don't think they'll strike till the crowd breaks up," said the girl, putting on the coat and slipping an automatic into the pocket. "By then it won't matter, as long as I'm not taken alive. Goodbye."

She turned round, did something to her face in front of the mirror, and put on the hat. When she swung back, Paradine had a frightening vision of himself standing there, a mirror-image, realising in the same second that the face was a rubber mask. He pulled her roughly towards him and kissed her, feeling the woman's body under the shabby raincoat, the warm lips behind the slit in the mask. Then she was gone.

Out in the tent, there was some applause and a mutter of voices, and Alexander came into the booth, mopping his brow. He stared at Paradine, his lardy face working in a kind of rage.

"A right bloody mess we're in now," he said. "This way, we've no time to lose, but it might just work."

They moved out into the night, past a tent that smelt rankly of animals, past a few dark caravans, to an elderly battered car. Alexander started the engine, which purred with unexpected quietness and power.

"What are we waiting for?" said Paradine.

"You'll see," said the magician, with the same suppressed rage.

Almost at once, on the far side of the fairground, whistles blew and a red very-light blazed in the dark. There was the flat sound of pistol-shots, followed by several hollow bursts of automatic fire. At the same time Alexander let in the clutch; the car jolted over some rough ground, swung out onto a road, and purred away.

"That was the girl, wasn't it?" said Paradine.

"It was. She died to give you a chance. I wish I could think you were worth it. You're all alike, you soft-bellied HQ amateurs. A girl like that was worth twenty of you."

In the dim moonlight, the plump man was leaning out to watch the streaking road; his white face was crumpled with tears and rage.

"She's dying there with her guts blown out for you. Don't you forget it."

"I won't," said Paradine.

There seemed nothing more to say. The road was rising steadily towards a dim gap in the hills ahead, and was now flanked by thick pine-woods. The freezing wind thrummed through the body-work of the old car; Paradine hunched himself close and concentrated on conserving body-temperature. Alexander seemed not to notice; sitting upright in his seedy magician's clothes, gripping the wheel with soiled white gloves, he had a power and dignity.

"Look behind," he said as they came up onto the shoulder of the first hill.

"Something on the road," said Paradine. "Two— three cars with dimmed lights. A fair way back but coming fast. They'll gain on us."

"How far?"

"Maybe a couple of miles."

"It's enough. Listen carefully, Paradine. Soon we come to a sharp bend, and the road starts to go down again. I'm going to slow down by a break in the woods on your side. Jump there and make straight through the break. There's a path there, narrow but clear. Follow it up as fast as you can till you get to the stone tower under the cliff. If you're lucky, you might find the Gespenster there. He's tricky and dangerous, but he's your only hope now. No, don't ask questions. Get ready. Now—" the car slowed on the sharp bend, and without turning his head, the magician shouted "—goodbye, amateur—jump."

Paradine opened the door and jumped, rolling over into a shallow ditch thick with pine-needles. In a single continuous movement, he was on his feet again, going at a stumbling run through the gap and up the path. He was well into the trees when three powerful cars roared along the road and disappeared.

He laboured on up the steep and almost-invisible path, tripping over roots, branches slashing at his face and hands. A fallen trunk caught him across the shins, and he sprawled full length and lay there, trying to bring his breathing under control. Beyond the hiss and roar of the wind in the pines, he caught a sound of prolonged gunfire, and a muffled explosion. It would not be very long before the searchers were coming back.

At last the trees thinned, and he came out onto the last steep track under the moonlight, with broken shale sliding and clattering under his feet. Above him loomed the edge of a sheer bluff, and, at its base, what appeared to be a mass of fallen debris. But as he climbed, and the shadowy outline changed, it took the form of a squat tower, built of huge stone blocks set against the base of the bluff. A light winked momentarily in the deepest part of the shadow; he felt his way through a narrow opening, stooped and squeezed along a passage, and entered a stone room in which a candle burned on a rough trestle-table.

The man behind the table was so tall that Paradine did not realise at first that he must be sitting down.

97

He was immense and square, with long arms that hung against his sides, the forearms laid parallel on the table, the huge square hands laid flat, palms down. His face was disquietingly long and straight; beneath the brim of his round flat hat, his heavy-lidded eyes did not blink.

When Paradine entered the stone chamber, the candle flickered and the huge square figure seemed to move, surrounded by wavering shadows. The mouth opened rhythmically and said:

"I am the Gespenster. Alexander sent you."

"Alexander is dead," said Paradine. "He said you might help me."

"Don't be afraid," said the harsh, level voice. "I am not dangerous, merely different. What do you want?"

"I need help. I have to steal the Troublemaker."

"Then I will help you."

"What is the Troublemaker?"

"A device for multiplying possibilities."

"I don't understand."

"Of course not. Listen, I will tell you some words. Freedom, choice, possibility, guilt, renunciation, decision, acceptance. Do they mean anything to you?"

"Nothing."

"I will try to explain. What is the basic law of the Universe?"

"Cause and effect."

"Quite so. To every effect, one cause. To every cause, one effect. No more, no less. You are hungry, you eat. You feel desire, you make love. You are threatened, you kill. Man is part of the necessary chain of cause and effect. Of course, the two societies which constitute our world interpret this differently. One says: leave all things free to follow their natural path, it must be that set out for them, and none other. The other says: since the law is the same for all men, we must identify it and obey it in unison. Both are basically the same, they obey Necessity. Now try to think of a universe in which a cause may have more than one effect, and a man must think and say which is to be, and which not to be."

"Such a place is unthinkable," said Paradine, trying in vain to think it.

"Here, yes. Now ask me your question again." The monumental figure stared at him, unmoving except for the lower jaw. The harsh voice remained dead level.

"What is the Troublemaker?" said Paradine, feeling his mouth go dry.

"A device for changing the laws of this universe. Once it is switched on, the unthinkable will happen."

"What must I do when I take it?"

"What is necessary," said the Gespenster, and fell silent for a long time. At last Paradine asked:

"How shall I take it?"

"I will tell you," said the Gespenster. Paradine listened carefully, and left the stone chamber. As soon as his footsteps died away outside, the shadows swirled up behind the impassive figure, and the candle went out.

Paradine followed the Gespenster's instructions, and found himself at last expertly backing a giant ore-transporter into one of the openings which ran along the base of the colossal factory. He set the controls so that the ore began to discharge into the automatic hopper, picked up a briefcase and left the cab of the transporter. Stripping off his brown coveralls he threw them into the hopper: underneath, he was wearing the green coveralls of a mechanic. He made sure that the appropriate security card was in the vest pocket, and walked into the long row of toilets. At the other end, he checked in with the guards, and took the escalator up to the next floor.

He entered the toilets, tore off the green coveralls and flushed the strips of soluble plastic down the lavatory. Underneath, he was wearing the blue coveralls of an electrician. At the other end, he checked in with the guards, using a new security card, and took the escalator up to the next floor.

Again he entered the toilets, tore off the blue coveralls and flushed them down the lavatory. Underneath he was wearing the grey coveralls of an overseer. At the other end, he checked in with the guards, used a new security card, and took the escalator up to the next floor.

Again he entered the toilets, tore off the grey coveralls and flushed them down the lavatory. Underneath, he was wearing the yellow coveralls of a junior production executive. At the other end, he checked in with the guards, using a new security card, and took the escalator up to the next floor.

Here he walked briskly and purposefully along a series of open galleries toward the other end of the building. Below him the various levels of the factory thrummed endlessly: night and day the shift-workers came and went, ore cascaded into crushers, bright metal flowed, dynamos whined, dropforges thudded, lathes screamed, profiling-machines chittered, conveyor-belts rumbled, cases were nailed and stencilled.

On the fifth floor, the finished products were displayed. Kraag, the leader. Kraag healing the sick. Kraag the discus-thrower. Kraag the harvester. Kraag in shining armour. Kraag the thinker. Kraag rewarding motherhood. Field Air Vice-Admiral Kraag, Cosmonaut Kraag. In all sizes, from heroic bronzes suitable for city squares, down to small pewter medallions intended for distribution at mass rallies. And at one end, filling the whole wall, a colossal head, its brutal features enlarged to the scale of mountains, rising from a plain base with the simple inscription KRAAG cut in leters one metre deep.

At first the vast head appeared of hardly more than human size, but as he approached it along the endless gallery, it rose steadily up until it loomed over him, its awful nostrils opening above him like canopies of darkness. Beneath the base, what had been a tiny black rectangle no bigger than an exclamation-mark was now the door of an elevator. He entered it and, as it rose, he tore off the yellow coveralls and hid them under the seat. Underneath, he was wearing the white coveralls of an artist. When the elevator reached the upper floor, he checked in with the guards, using a new security card, and walked quickly down the corridor. He found the store-room and the disused service-duct, up which he inched his way, using the miniature magnetic grapples. Half-way up, he opened his wrist-detector, and used it to set the three dome-shaped devices which blanked out the whole alarm system.

When he emerged from the duct, he entered a large square room, evenly and brightly lit, quite empty except for the Troublemaker which stood on a platform in the middle of the room. It was not much larger than a carry-case, and he lifted it easily in one hand. It had no visible means of opening, and beside the handle there was a single red push-button under a sealed plastic hood.

He had taken three steps with it when the alarm-siren went off with a roar which shook the floor and made his teeth ache, and he realised that the protective devices had been tampered with. The end wall of the room slammed up out of sight, and along the outer corridor raced a green electrocar from the front of which protruded the stubby barrel of a nerve-cannon. The gunner, a tall albinoid, swung round in his bucket-seat as he brought the cannon to bear on Paradine, and his pink eyes blazed with joy and fury.

There was a last defence. Paradine wrenched off the plastic hood, and leaned forward with body tensed. Even as the intolerable fires of the nerve-gun washed through him, he collapsed onto the Trouble-maker, his chest thudding home on the red button.

The room blinked out, blinked on again. The albinoid guard, the nerve-cannon, the tower, the colossal head and myriad statues of Kraag, the dismal fairground and the sleet-riddled town blinked out, blinked on again. The globe, its star, the apparent universe blinked on and on into a rapid strobic flicker, in which masses and outlines softened and dissolved. Paradine decided that he must have time to think about it, and between one blink and the next, he found time enough.

SIX

For a long time, or even before a long time, it simply was, formless, static, undreaming. When it became aware of itself, it was conscious of two things, simplicity and potentiality. It was too simple to be of interest, yet it contained infinite possibilities; it must explore itself and thrust out, each in turn, along the line of those possibilities; yet in order to do so, it must also limit itself, become itself.

It limited itself. The nothing around it became darkness; the emptiness solidified into a nutrient medium; the darkness became warmth and light. It spun out the complex organic molecular chains, and made itself a single floating cell, and divided and differentiated, until the waters became milky with its presence. It began to create structures, to feed on itself. It invented sex, which had possibilities. Presently there were corals and sponges, and bony creatures that scuttled among rocks, and fish that swam and grew, the greater devouring the less, feeding the cruel intelligence that looked out through small dead eyes and blood-hungry senses.

It drove up onto the land, breathed air, spawned in the warm sand, fed, grew, proliferated. All the time it was aware in itself on the dim slow murmur of green life, which spread and grew up towards the sun in vast forests, rank with vitality and decay. Across the swamps and bayous and into the lush lowlands it dreamed on, of raw life in the form of lizards, large as floating or walking islands, or swift and terrible, fanged or winged or horned or plated.

It had reached the limits of mere life; it drew in again upon itself. The world became colder. With a sudden quickening of the senses, it thrust out again, warm-blooded, bearing and caring for its young; and it fed on a new world of sharp discreet objects, of light and darkness, of shape and colour, of smells and sounds, of pleasure and pain. It scented its way delicately across thyme and pine-forests; it sank its teeth deliciously into the throat of fresh prey; it roused to the iridescent plumage of the courting male; it stitched across the twilight of a web of faintest sounds.

It was aware of itself now thrusting out along a myriad lines of force, but chiefly of the one on which it could grasp the flaked stone in prehensile fingers, knowing that it was itself and not the stone, or the tree, or the mate, or the sun.

Then it withdrew, undifferentiating itself, and becoming all the living creature at rest. It knew what was itself and what not itself; and in doing so, it became aware of another, strange and dangerous. To find and meet it, it acted swiftly, drawing on its repertory of forms, and improvised a fantasy. With golden breast and turquoise scales, with cloudy hair streaming in the undersea currents, with fastidious webbed hands and snub nostrils that sluiced water through her hidden gills, Sea-Helena swam swiftly down through the golden, the green, the aquamarine and the blue midnight of undersea glittering with cold phosphorescent stars.

The statue was almost hidden among the tall wavering tangle of leathery weed, and at first she could only feel her way towards it, the sensitive detector in her mind sensing out the violent life imprisoned within it. When she swept aside the last wavering brown curtain of weed, it revealed itself as a squat brutal structure of a man, carved in grey stone, immeasurably old and eroded, crusted with molluscs and feathery sea-mosses. The blunt head was thrust back and the blank eyes stared up at the shifting blue light above; the knotted arms and fists were drawn down, and the figure crouched, as if its shape had adapted itself to the life that raged in its imprisonment deep within it. The life was thwarted, violent, blind; it did not know its own power. On the base of the statue, half obliterated by the drifting sand, was incised the word KRAAG.

She let her mind play around it curiously. She knew no life that was not her own; ugly as this life was, it was other, and she wished to know what it might prove to be. Let it be changed, little by little; living substance taking over, until the stone became no more than a rigid exoskeleton, a jointed stony armour. With a rasp, the head turned and looked about. The figure straightened from its crouch, and, stepping down from the pedestal, began to move across the seabed, tearing and beating aside the weed as it went.

She followed it, still curious, swimming slowly and delicately along as it plunged clumsily in clouds of stirred-up sand and mud, towards the shallows and the shore. On the edge of a wide bay, lit by a glaring yellow sunset, it paused on the edge of the tide before trudging on, inland, across the dunes and onto the sloping uplands.

She dissolved herself and drifted in a thick scatter of golden foam across the wash of the incoming sea. The off-shore wind tumbled it all together, and in the last of the sunlight it gathered itself into a tall golden woman who strode up the beach with the last of the sea cascading down her haunches, and passed among the whispering sea grasses, and disappeared into the dusk.

On the high headland which reached out to enclose the bay from the north, the dark line of a solitary tower stood up against the fading bar of the sunset. A point of light shone out steadily from the window of the upper chamber. A shadowy figure stood motionless on the flat roof, staring out over the crumbling battlement at the last of the fierce yellow light in the eastern sky. Already dark fingers of cloud were beginning to claw their way across it; a chill wind sprang up, and the sea moaned and hushed.

Seth Paradine drew his fur mantle more closely about him and pulled up the hood. He adjusted the astrolabe, and turned to where Oloboolian, the Lady of the Night, high in the eastern sky, like a small intense green moon, swam into her full magnificence. She stood now full in the constellation of the Hippocamp; but below and to her left lay a point of red phosphorescence, like a splinter of ruby. This was

Voord, the wandering planet whose long eccentric orbit wove right through those of the other five; Voord, which must some day collide with and destroy the world; Voord, whose rare appearance in the sky portended the alien and the uncovenanted.

Finishing his observation, he turned and paced slowly across the flagstones, a tall dark-cowled figure, towards the narrow spiral staircase which led down to the study. Here, in this lofty room with its irregular stone walls, its stacks of heavy leather-bound books, its racks of alembics, its stills and furnaces, its star-maps and tables of the elements, its dark crannies strewn with scrolls, amulets, Geiger-counters, coloured flasks, microscopes and rats' nests, he had completed the studies which had made him an adept. Here he had communed with spirits, invented the structure of the atom, discovered DNA and perfected the Philosopher's Stone and the Elixir of Life. Here he was about to achieve the last degree of mastery; he would make life. Having done that, and attained his own immortality, he would be free to retire to the summit of the tower and pass into that last absorbing act of contemplation, in which the body would become nothing and the mind all, fixed in an ecstatic ageless contemplation of the universe, until time itself came to a stop.

The moment of conjunction was approaching. He coded his latest observations and fed them into the computer, together with the penultimate words of power. He passed slowly along the bench where stood his first tentatives, the tiny homunculi, some dreaming, some frenziedly active, in their warm prisons of glass. They were the toys of his youth, childish but lovable—the musician-prince with his little tinkling harp; the spider-woman who had eaten her mate; the idiot-girl, bald and yellow; the spangled juggler perpetually whirling his indian-clubs; the knight, like a small iron statue; the duchess making eyes at the tattered beggar in the next jar; the sleep-walker; the washerwoman; the siamese-twins; the black boxer sparring with his own shadow; the girl who sang perpetually on one note amid the shining golden waterfall of her hair. After tonight, he must put them away.

A blast of wind rustled the hangings and the rats squeaked and pattered in the shadows. The golden girl sang in her glass cage like a fly on the pane. The computer chattered out the final calculations. Paradine turned to the great east window which framed the two planets, the green and the red; they appeared now to be almost touching, like some weird binary. But even as he watched for the moment of conjunction, a great fist of cloud seemed to enclose them, and from its knuckles dripped lightning. A long hollow mutter of thunder rolled out above the roaring of the sea.

It was time. From its niche beside the Stone he drew out the crystal phial which corruscated with shifting points of light; from it, he drew up the exactly measured amount into the hypodermic.

The masterwork lay on the operating table in the centre of the room, a single bright light burning above it. He hesitated for a moment, calming the excitement in his soul, before flinging off the sheet with a swift movement. Lying on the operating table was the naked body of a man. He was of heroic size, with the thighs and biceps of an ancient prize fighter, and a massive arch of chest. The chin was deep and square, the nose jutting, the brow high and ample. All this he had created, isolating the vital atoms from plant and beast, forming the frame in his furnaces and shaping the organs, labouring long over the delicate convolutions of the brain. Only at the last, as he moulded the herculean body in the casting-vat, had an intrusion occurred. He had suddenly seen a golden woman come up out of the surf and stride away into the hills, and for an instant his concentration had flickered, just as it came to the moulding of the head. The seams and scars which thus appeared on the face gave it the look of some time-eroded statue, ageless and mysteriously dignified.

The computer-set chronometer buzzed warningly. There was a roar of surf and a scream of wind. As he raised the hypodermic, he saw the specks of light moving faster and faster within it, and the reflection of lightning. The buzzer sounded again; he drove home the long hollow needle and injected directly into the heart, while thunder rolled from every quarter of the sky.

"It is done," he said aloud, nearly fainting as he leaned forward with his hands gripping the edge of the table. A flush of colour crept over the marble whiteness of the recumbent figure, the great arched chest fluttered and began to rise and fall majestically. The carved eyelids blinked and opened and wrinkled up as the eyes peered out short-sightedly upon the world. The figure sneezed enormously, and sat up. He draped over its shoulders a loose white robe and led it gently to a chair, where it sat like an ancient emperor, with its vast swathed body and its noble flawed face. He held a glass of cordial to its lips; it took the glass from him, swallowed it down, and sighed appreciatively.

"Claret," it said in a voice like the echo of thunder, "is the liquor for boys, port for men, but he who aspires to be a hero must drink brandy."

"What am I to call you" said Paradine.

"John Samuelson," said the figure firmly.

"You are now alive, John Samuelson. Does it give you pleasure to be alive?"

"To talk is good and to laugh is good," said the figure, holding out its glass to be replenished. "A tavern-chair is the throne of human felicity."

"Then what is the purpose of life?"

The figure rolled about in distress, and the seamed face crumpled. "The whole of life . . . is . . . but keeping away the thoughts . . . of death."

"Is there no choice?"

"Nature sets her gifts on the right hand and on the left," said the figure more calmly.

"Are not all things possible to the mind?"

"We may take fancy for our companion but we must let reason be our guide. All power of fancy over reason is a degree of insanity."

"By what then will you rule your life?"

The figure started to its feet and its voice rolled out

in full thunder. "Give me something to desire," it shouted, staring with blank eyes towards the east, suddenly cold and rigid, a heroic statue eroded by the ages. The tower and the granite cliffs beneath it quivered with spasms of earthquake. His mind shaking and churning, Paradine rushed to the great window, where the storm had cleared and left the two planets again exposed, the green one just below the red.

With a hissing roar they rushed up into the sky and burst into a rain of golden fire. Others followed, and the sky was full of flaming and whirling stars and the flat explosions of bursting rockets. Below him the whole curve of the shore twinkled with lights, some still, some moving; a line of lights stretched out into the bay and others, doubled by reflection, danced on the calm gently-moving waters.

Sombre in his enfolding robes, Paradine swept along the broad promenade which now followed the curve of the bay. On one side the tall hotels towered up in domes and pinnacles, with lights glowing softly in the dining rooms, with orchestras in gold-frogged uniforms of blue or scarlet playing polkas and waltzes, with tall moustachio'd commissionaires gravely waiting on the carriages. Along the broad carriage way, open landaus swept by, bearing gentlemen in white ties with the stars of exotic orders glittering on their breasts, and ladies whose white necks and arms and high-piled hair glittered with pearls and diamonds. Along the sea-front coloured lanterns were strung between the palms, and from the yachts across the water floated the sound of violins. On the massive pier rose the starlit domes of the casino, through whose windows could be seen slow-moving figures grouped about the green baize tables; while from a service entrance, a dark bundle was being discreetly huddled into a closed carriage. The air was full of the scent of mimosa and the popping of champagne corks and the rattle of roulette wheels.

A man leaned over the terrace-balustrade of the largest and most luminous of all the hotels. His opera-hat was tilted far back on his flamboyantly white hair and his pink eyes looked out merrily on the world. Paradine sensed that this was the other, the centre of all this otherness which had so suddenly over-whelmed and brought to ruin the noble work of his solitude in the tower. He glared up at him accusingly.

"You," he said, "are the earthquake in my mind."

"Don't know about that, old boy," said the white-haired man cheerfully. "Come up and have some bubbly."

He beckoned Paradine up the broad steps and led him to a table on which stood two large silver cham-pagne-buckets, one filled with banknotes, the other with a jeroboam of champagne bedded in crushed ice, together with an ice-swan whose hollow back was filled with caviare.

"Nothing but the best, old boy," said the albino. "Fill 'em up, garçon, there's plenty more where that came from. Cin-chin, old boy."

Paradine tasted the cold wine and his mind rocked again. "You are the earthquake in my mind," he said wonderingly, "you."

"Sounds a bit woozy to me, old chap. Here, have some more champers, and try some of this fishpaste stuff with it, tastes marvellous."

"You have undone the noble work of centuries," said Paradine.

"Tommyrot, old boy. I've just broken the bank again. For the fifth time. Head croupier bally well shot himself because of the disgrace. Jolly sporting of him, I call it. *Noblesse oblige*, and all that, what?"

"Now I have nothing," shouted Paradine. "Must I shoot myself too? Must I fling myself from the top of the tower? Give me something to desire," he thun-dered in the voice of old Samuelson.

"What? Oh that's all arranged, old fellow. And here they are now." A crowd of dancing girls ran squealing and cooing up the stairway, and the lights gleamed mellowly on their white powdered shoulders, their bosoms bursting out of slender corsets, their long smooth legs and tiny slippers. Their doll faces, dark and fair, were alive with fierce and simple greed as they flung themselves at the albino, kissing him—

"Billy daarling ... Billy chéri ... Billy liebling ... Billy honey ... Billy bambino ... I loove you ... ich liebe ... j'aime ... amo ... blond beast ... quel animal ... barbaro ..."—flung themselves at the champagne, the caviare, the great mounds of food wheeled up on trolleys by a procession of waiters.

"What did I tell you, old friend? Billy thinks of everything." He sprinkled them lightly with banknotes. "Take your pick, it's all on me."

The girls squealed and tussled over the champagne, the food, the money.

"What is the holy father doing here?" asked a dark girl.

"To marry us, what else?" shouted Billy with a roar of laughter. "And we'll all sail away to the coast of Barbary and I'll buy you a sultan's palace to live in." They squealed and cooed and kissed him, but continued to glance coldly at the cowled figure of Paradine.

"Silly lovelies," said Billy, "have you forgotten the masquerade? It's carnival night, mardi gras, you know, what?" He jumped upon the table and yelled: "Carnival! it's the car-ni-vaaal!" His voice echoed across the bay; there was a sudden hush, broken by the roar of rockets filling the sky and the dark reflecting water.

"Of course, it's the carnival ... bliss ... but how original ... Billy has *loovely* friends ..." Half the girls flung themselves at Paradine; predatory little hands plucked at the furred robes, hot little mouths pressed themselves to his with excited hiccups.

From the terraces of the hotels and along the broad esplanade swarmed a crowd of costumed revellers— swathed in oriental silks, armoured, bird-feathered, demon-headed—and the orchestras came down and fell into step among them, and the air was filled with dazzling confetti and balloons. Billy and his girls joined an endless snake-dance line and were whisked away among the crowd, beneath the men on stilts and the enormous nodding clown-masks. Paradine whirled along in the crowd, through explosions of colour and trumpets, sequined dominoes screaming, swollen idiot-heads, until the myriad-moving crowd spun him out again among the palm trees by the shore.

Below him on the sands stood a striped tent, with a sign over the entrance in flourishing gold letters: Madame Gerpenster, Clairvoyant Extraordinary. Stirred by dim memories, he lifted the flap and entered. An old woman was sitting at a table, a shining globe between her hands. Her old face was dry and brittle like a death-mask, and came alive only in the bright black eyes and in the movement of the jaw when she spoke. With her coloured kerchief and bright shapeless clothes and brittle face, she might or must have strayed down here out of the carnival. The jaw moved and the creaking voice said:

"Welcome, pretty gentleman, old granny's been waiting for you since you came down from your tall house on the hill."

"You know me?"

"I know all about you."

"Who am I? Whence do I come?"

"You come from that which is into that which is not; you go to that which may be."

"You tell me nothing, old granny. Your words have no meaning."

"Not to you, pretty gentleman, not to you. Listen, I will tell you some more words. Necessity, law, cause, effect, logic, consequence, acceptance, purpose. Do they mean anything to you?"

"Nothing, old granny."

"I will try to explain. What is the basic principle of the universe?"

"There is no principle but the will. What I believe is true."

"But you know now that what another believes is also true. Can there be two truths, or many?"

"That has troubled me. Can it be that the other lives also in a forgotten corner of my mind?"

The jaw dropped and the old woman cackled.

"In my glass I see the dark and the bright of the mind locked each in each, like the dark and bright of the moon. If what you believe is true, then a man may desire wisdom or pleasure, and in the end they will be no more than the same thing."

"You are no more than another part of my mind," said Paradine. "Tell me what I must do now."

The old woman suddenly shrieked with laughter. "The tower! the tower! it is falling! you must go at once to the tower!"

In a swirl of dark robes, he rushed from the tent and up onto the esplanade. Behind him, the old woman billowed to the floor, a painted mask and a flutter of bright silks, and with a soft plop the crystal ball turned to water and dribbled over the table.

Among the crowds on the esplanade, massive floats passed along, carrying masked revellers and mounds of flowers.

"Hallo there, old boy, I thought we'd lost you. Climb up, we're going to have an orgy."

Dressed in the purple robes of an emperor, with a chaplet of gilded leaves on his white hair, Billy beamed down on him from a throne on the largest and highest of the floats. Sweating waiters draped in bath-towels poured endless champagne. The girls, in floating transparent draperies, pelted the crowd with grapes and roseleaves.

"It's the holy man," they screamed, helping him up "... petit monstre ... schreck ... bruto ... I *loove* the smell of incense ..."

"There's a jolly old tower up on the hill—just the place for a bit of a bash, what?" shouted Billy. "Whip 'em up, driver!"

The heavy horses which drew the float broke into an astonishing gallop, and the whole contraption dashed along the esplanade, shedding grapes, roses, bottles and towelled waiters. The girls clung screaming around the rocking throne, as if they were about to be slaughtered for the funeral of a barbaric king.

"No!" screamed Paradine. "No! you cannot take the tower—it is the citadel of my soul, the fortress of my mind! From it I—and I alone—make and remake the world."

"Don't talk such rot, old boy. Here, have some of this lovely bubbly."

The float creaked and strained wildly up the broad curved cliff-road, and stopped below the tower. Behind them halted a procession of hansom-cabs from which swarmed more waiters bearing crates of champagne and hampers of delicious cold food, which the girls began to eat with screams of pleasure.

"Greedy little devils," said Billy, striking them with a small whip, "get into the tower."

Paradine sprang up the steps and barred the doorway with outstretched arms.

"You may not enter here! I abolish you! I unthink you! Begone with the phantoms of the night! Look, the sun is rising in the west."

Billy glanced impatiently at the bar of light along the horizon.

"Bosh, old boy. It's rising in the east, never rises anywhere else."

Paradine felt the earth turning giddily beneath him as it spun end-over-end.

"You shall not enter!" he shouted.

"Who wants your rotten old tower, anyway?" said Billy pettishly. "Look."

He plunged his hand into the massive stonework and pulled away a great handful of greyish fibrous stuff, which he flung on the ground. "Come on, girls." The girls rushed up giggling and began to tear away the tower in armfuls, while the waiters scuttled about protecting the food and drink. The whole of the tall grim-looking structure began to sway and topple above them, and slid down with a whoosh in a great cloud of dust and nothing more. Everyone began to sneeze.

"Look at him!" said Billy, as he staggered about, sneezing and laughing, "You're just a bally old fraud, holy man. Look at him, girls, he's a fraud."

The girls turned on him, chattering in high voices, clutching with their little claws at the rich furred robes, which tore away into long floating strips, like dusty cobweb. He began to run down the hill, and they all screamed at him and pelted him with chick-

113

en-bones and empty bottles. A champagne-glass broke on the path and gashed his feet cruelly, but he stumbled on in pain and terror, away from the headland, out beyond the town, until the dunes gave way to desert, and he collapsed mumbling among the tall dancing dust-devils.

Leaving wreckage behind him, Billy, dressed now in striped blazer and flannels and straw-boater, came prancing down the hill in the midst of his girls.

"Come along, kiddies," he called. "The yacht's waiting. I think it's time I invented the Jazz Age."

The sun blared like brass out of the sky; the night came down with lunar cold; Paradine staggered on across the desert, roasted and freezing, for many days. He licked the night-dew from the rocks; he sucked scraps of meat from splintered bones left by jackals; he chewed the bark of stunted bushes and scrabbled beneath them for grubs. His hair and beard grew long and matted; his body became as lean and hard and shrunken as smoked meat.

At last he came to the place where even the rocks and the bones ceased, and there was nothing but endless low hills of dust. The sun blazed down, and the whole empty landscape became a vast heat-shimmer, which played strange tricks on his seared eye-balls. Sometimes it would slow down, and across the desolation would flicker other things which could not be; the control deck of a space-ship, endless void, fiery birds, a fairground, a two-headed giant, men fighting in snow, old newspapers, and always his own body tumbling forward onto the case with its red activator-button. Then it would speed up, becoming a strobic flicker; and this at last passed upward into a high shrill sound and darkness.

When he awoke, the flicker was there, slow and gentle, and the sound had eased into a fluctuating musical murmur. He sat up on a grassy bank. Above him tall palm trees towered into the air, with the sunlight twinkling and moving between the cross-laced stems and the broad flickering leaves. A little spring trickled down among rocks, feeding a green

114

pool below. On a stone beside him stood a jug of water, beaded with cold drops, a loaf of coarse bread and a bunch of dates. Slowly he ate and drank, then lay down again and slept.

He dreamed, and in his dream he rose up and walked to the pool. On the other side of it, partly hidden among leaves, was a small white domed building, with narrow steps leading down into the green water. He waited, and presently the surface of the pool was disturbed, and a tall golden woman walked out of the water and up the steps into the temple. Without knowing why, he waded out into the pool, and washed and purified himself, and walked up the steps also.

Inside, the building was square and plain with a low doorway on the further side; cool light and air washed into it from the slits under the dome. Dressed in a robe of dark stuff, the golden woman stood before a long embroidery-frame, her fingers going incredibly swiftly with the needle, pausing only briefly as she reached for one of the many bobbins of coloured silk that hung along the bottom of the frame. She paid no attention to his coming; there was no sound except the faint click and scratch of the needle in the fabric.

Curious, he looked along the pictured web. First there was a complex pattern of every kind of beast, bird and fish, plant and tree. These led on until they seemed to cluster and find their significance in the embroidered figure of the golden woman herself. From there onward, the web became obscure; it seemed to tell a series of stories, some in pictures, some in a picture-writing in which the wavy lines of water and the symbols of male power and of motherhood appeared in various forms. There was the tower on the headland and himself in his initiate's robes; and there was the albino Billy with his girls. Then both of them reappeared, mixed up somehow with the water-symbol, and he saw a little picture of himself emerging from the pool, and the male-female symbols, and something that stood for power, or fear, or the unknown. Now she was working on a horse and—flick,

flick, went the shining needle, and the bobbins of silk clicked as she moved them—it was a great black horse with fiery eyes, and on its back was a fierce bearded rider whose black robes swirled about him like thunderclouds. Satisfied with it, she stabbed her needle into the bland web and turned to him.

"I saw you from the tower," he said, "when you came up out of the sea. Now you are part of my dream."

"No, you are part of my dream," she said.

"I am the dreamer. I am asleep by the pool."

"Your dream is only a part of mine, a dream within a dream." She pointed to the long web of embroidery. "That is the matrix of my dream. So much you may see; but if you look at it again, you will reenter it. You have sought the wisdom of the stars and of the spirit: stay with me and I will teach you the wisdom of the earth and of the body. While you are with me, the two dreams are one. Come."

Taking him by the hand, she led him through the low doorway into the inner sanctuary, where she initiated him into the mysteries.

He stayed there with her for three days, and she taught him in dream-songs, how first of all there was the One, and how it embodied itself in the all-mothering ocean, from which all things came and to which all things would return. On the fourth day he awoke to find himself alone, and the door open, and he could see her walking slowly down the steps into the pool. The web was longer now, and stretched all along the wall of the temple. With terrible curiosity, he walked softly towards it, and found that the bearded man had now become the leader of many, riding across the desert towards a white city. He touched the web: the building trembled, and the dome crumbled in a shower of dust, letting in a harsh blaze of sunlight. At the touch of the sun, the embroidered web shrivelled into grey rags.

He ran to the entrance of the ruined temple; a few slimy crumbling steps led down into the pool, now green with scum; starved palm trees drooped among
116

the rocks. Across the desert, filtered and swollen through red evening light, came a cloud of dust and a muffled drumming of hooves.

Paradine stumbled back across the broken pavement of the temple. The further door had rotted from its hinges, and the inner shrine was no more than broken walls. The advance guard reined up by the oasis in a great flurry of dust, men in loose white robes, veiled to the eyes, who carried swords and short bows and rode small tough horses. The leader dismounted and, kneeling by the pool, raised his veil, scooped up a mouthful of water, and spat.

"It'll do for the horses," he said. "Tell the Khan we camp here tonight. You others, spread out and search."

Presently the main body of the horsemen came up at an easier pace. Peering through the broken doorways, Paradine could see the towering figure of the horseman in black, for whom all made way. Then came the huntsmen with their great lean hounds, and the camel-train carrying the women and children and the stores; the evening din of the camp went up, as tents were set up and pickets hammered into the hard ground, and fires of dry thorn and camel-dung began to glow and crackle in the dusk. He drew further back into the shadows.

A crowd of tattered white-robed men carrying bales and bundles came clambering into the broken temple. They flung out the rubbish; some scrambled up the walls on each side and hung a wide striped awning between them; others spread faded woollen rugs and worn cushions and small tables all over the floor, and set up smoking oil-lamps on stands and braziers of glowing charcoal. In an instant, the ruined building was full of raffish golden light and gaudy faded colours and tattered finery.

Stripped of their masking veils, the faces of the men were dark and vivid, and they laughed with loud teeth as they quickly spread the furniture about. But the laughter stopped as Khan Kraag strode in, immense, black and scowling. He struck the dust from his black robes and rinsed his hands and mouth in a

117

bowl of water offered by a kneeling servant. Then he flung himself down on a pile of cushions and picked moodily at a bunch of withered dates, while his warriors stood around muttering and sniffing hopefully for the smell of supper.

The clatter of the cooks in the inner room was broken by a sudden cry and scuffle. The chief cook, a lardy pock-faced fellow of uncertain temper, appeared suddenly in the doorway; he held Paradine by the neck and ran him out into the room.

"Great Khan," he panted, "there's an old goat we found hiding here, he claims to be a holy man; for all I know, he may be a fool and a bard as well, to tumble and sing for you over supper."

And he sent Paradine spinning into the middle of the room, where he collapsed in a heap on the carpet, which smelt of dust and dried camel-dung. The Khan leaned forward in his seat and tapped him with his whip.

"Well, holy man, what do you seek?"

"I—I—I seek wisdom, great Khan."

"I could use some wisdom, holy man. Did you find any? Where did you search?"

"I studied the wisdom of the books. I knew all the secrets of the earth and air, the waters and the stars. I made gold. I made life."

"And was this wisdom?"

"No, great Khan. Another came who sought pleasure in wealth and women, and all my wisdom turned to dust."

"More fool than holy man. What else?"

"I found a woman, and more than a woman. She lived here, I thought, in this temple. She taught me that all life comes from the One who dwells in the waters, and returns there again."

"And was this wisdom?"

"No, great Khan. It was a dream—nothing."

And if it was a dream, he thought, it was a dream within my dream. Then let these bearded savages have a place in my dream also, so that through them I may destroy my destroyer.

"You are a fool, holy man," said the Khan. "Look at

118

you, you are thin and hairy like a monkey; and all you own is a dirty loincloth. Is this wisdom?"

Crouched on the dusty threadbare carpet, Paradine thought to himself: and what do you own? these ragged tents, these wild poor people and starved beasts? if this is the best you can do, I can do better, and you shall serve in my dream, not I in yours. Twisting his head sideways to squint up into the ferocious bearded face, he said quickly:

"Perhaps there is another wisdom, great Khan, a wisdom of the desert."

"Tell."

"There is no wisdom in old books, which turn to dust, nor in pleasure which is soft and kills, not in the waters of a dream. But out of the desert comes hard wisdom, the wisdom of strength and power.

"You have wisdom, great Khan, to know and do. There are dwellers in cities who wear soft clothes and are fearful for their soft bodies. There are priests in temples who fatten on mysteries. There are warriors who faint for the kiss of steel. There are perfumed women with the claws of vultures." He dragged himself to his feet, still feeling the rawness from the broken glass. "They are like sheep bleating for the butcher's knife, great Khan. Let the sword strike them, and all their soft wealth be taken from them." He spun around shrieking. "Out of the desert comes strength in a tower of dust and wisdom in a fiery sword! Burn! sack! ravage! gouge! slice! impale! ravish! flay! quarter! pillage! ruin!" His eyes rolled up and he pitched back among the cushions, the slack mouth moving and mumbling.

The Khan stood up and looked around the assembly, seeing everywhere the smile of greed, the glitter in the eye.

"Get out," he said softly. "I will talk to the holy man when he awakes." And he sat down patiently beside Paradine, who seemed to writhe and mutter among the faded cushions.

Billy Merganser had rearranged his pleasure-city several times, but never found it quite satisfactory. He tried it with jazzbands and speakeasies; he tried it with honeycomb blocks of flats; he experimented with funfairs and swimmingpools, neonlights and poker-machines. None of them were improvements. Finally he decided to become gracefully middleaged and to revert to a simpler and more lasting style.

The elaborate artificial seafront ran like melted wax. A city of low massive white buildings stretched along the shore. Gentle surf creamed across the broad white beach, and the fishing boats swept home at evening to the inner harbour behind the breakwater. The narrow dark streets of the inner city huddled around the harbour, a place of broken lights, outcries, snatches of song, a cosily vicious huddle of sailors' dives, strip-joints and opium-dens. Billy was rather fond of it—some of his best girls were there—though he preferred to live in a huge cool house set in gardens beyond the outer boulevards, where he could swim in his marble pool and at night watch the fireflies among the oleanders. At the bottom of the gardens ran the old city ramparts, still largely intact; beyond them stretched the irrigated fields, and, on the rim of the horizon, the desert.

Lounging in red silk pyjamas, Merganser drank his morning coffee on the tree-shaded terrace that looked out beyond the town. He was pleased with the world he had made; life was good, the girls were better than ever, and even the climate had worked out right. Yet he yawned hugely, and remembered what that dotty chap had shouted: "Give me something to desire." Life was dull.

The cloud out of the desert was at first no more than a dirty fingerprint on the clear horizon. He sat up and watched it as it grew swiftly and came running in across the green fields, until he could discern the small energetic shapes of galloping horsemen, and the flutter of a wide yellow flag. Soon they reined up and the dust settled about them, fierce white-robed figures who sat their horses and stared up at the high broken battlements, while another slower cloud lumbered up in the distance.

He went quickly to the telephone, and summoned

the militia, which consisted of thirty-five bandsmen, twelve musketeers, three gunners and a splendid brass cannon used for firing salutes on his birthday. As an after-thought, he also called out the gendarmerie and the firebrigade. They made an impressive enough sight, strung out along the battlements, with the morning sun gleaming on the scarlet and blue and the white horsehair plumes, and twinkling on gold lace and brass helmet, on cuirasse and kettledrum.

The ranks of horsemen opened, and through the midst of them rode an enormous black-robed blackbearded man on a black horse. Behind him on a white donkey came a smaller figure, gaunt, tanned to mummy-flesh by the sun, clothed in a breech-clout and his own long hair. Leaping from his donkey, he rushed out in front of the host and began to jump about, gesticulating and shouting. Fragments of his words came to Merganser on the breeze: " . . . woe to the unclean city . . . filth and ordure . . . woe . . . woe . . . dashed against the wall . . . woe . . . eaten by hogs . . . fire and destruction . . . hurricane out of the desert . . . not a stone upon a stone . . . owls and bats . . . wild dogs . . . basilisks . . . woe . . . woe . . ."

He stopped suddenly on a shriek, extended arms quivering over the city. The black leader raised his arm, and the ranked horsemen stirred. The militia were the first to leave the wall, abandoning even their instruments, closely followed by the firemen and the gendarmerie. Merganser was left foolishly alone on the wall, watching the horsemen as they veered and poured along below him and thronged in through the wide gap where the old city gate had been torn down to make a highway. As he passed, the withered holy man could be heard yelling: "Slay them all, the Lord will know his own."

As the mass of horsemen careered along the broad boulevards and fanned out into the side streets, there was a certain amount of screaming, and here and there smoke billowed up. But the desert-riders became tired of stravaging about; they were a thrifty people, and it seemed wasteful to destroy the fine buildings, all with an excellent water supply, and

121

containing prodigious quantities of consumer goods. Someone was needed to supply necessary services and to transport the loot, and the local people, men and women, were prepared to be accommodating.

Magistrates and prominent citizens were driven to the central plaza and quartered, their broiled members distributed to various parts of the city for disciplinary purposes. Apart from this, by midafternoon, relative calm had returned. The Khan had set up a temporary headquarters on a great pile of cushions under a silken canopy in the plaza. The holy man crouched by the fountain, and sulked.

There was a sudden scuffle under the arcade and a party of guards appeared, led by the one-eyed huntsman and dragging a tall albino dressed in the rags of a pair of red silk pyjamas.

"Great Khan," panted the huntsman, "we caught this wretch trying to sneak away on a stolen horse. One said that he is the ruler of this wicked rich city. Shall we broil and quarter him, Khan?"

Khan Kraag was about to raise an indolent hand in permission, when the holy man leapt to his feet, crying: "This is truly the one, great Khan, the prince of pleasure, the lord of uncleanness, the scent of whose abomination goes up perpetually to heaven. Destroy him, great Khan, let him die in vileness and the earth be made clean."

One of Billy's pink eyes was half-closed by a heavy blow, but the other peered out at the world with sudden impudence. Bowing in his gaudy rags, he cried out gaily: "Greetings, great Khan. Why did you not of your courtesy send me a messenger to tell of your coming? I could have arranged a welcome suited to so exalted a ruler."

"Smite him! flay him! tear out his false tongue!" shouted the holy man.

"It is not too late for me to make amends, great Khan," said the albino quickly. "My palace is at your disposal, and its secret treasury, known only to myself. And then there are certain places in the old city, and those who live in them would do anything for my honoured guest, anything at all."

"Boil him in wine! choke him with molten gold! tear him apart with wild horses!" shrilled the holy man, but his voice was hoarse and weary.

"You interest me, Pink Eye," said Khan Kraag contemptuously. "I have a holy man, but no major domo. If I come to your old city, I shall bring my bodyguard."

"There is plenty for all," said Merganser politely.

The holy man collapsed gibbering in the dust beside the fountain.

"You shall tell me more about this as I eat," said the Khan, rising. "Have you good cooks?"

"Superb ones, great Khan."

"Good. Then at last I can hang my own cook. Pay no attention to the holy man, he is in a trance. No doubt when he awakes he will tell us all about his dreams."

Paradine's dreams merged with the shifting mirages of the desert and the bright flicker of the Troublemaker, in the midst of which the grinning face of Merganser and the brutal face of Kraag stared down at him. His mind like a screen darkened down to black, and in one corner a small round picture appeared and irised-in until it became the whole scene. The city had changed again, into a place of battlements and heavy gables.

With chanting and with holy banners, with incense and with the rhythmic scourging of penitential backs, the long procession of cowled figures wound into the square. In the midst, guarded by stalwart laybrothers armed with cudgels, came the procession of the condemned in their weird carnival robes and tall hats painted with flames and devils. Most of them could shuffle along in their leg-irons; some, who had needed closer questioning, were dragged along roped to hurdles, groaning as they bumped over the cobblestones.

The black files wound slowly round the square, past the ranks of pikemen representing the secular arm, around the tall iron stakes and the manacles and the orderly piles of faggots, the dry and the green, to the open space before the dais. There sat Cardinal Kraag, enormous in his scarlet robes, with the shrivelled figure of the black-robed black-bearded Inquisitor sitting at his feet on a low stool, symbol of humility.

The procession halted; the chanting stopped; the banners were furled; and the indictments were read out. Then the Cardinal rose like a fiery cloud and rolled out the anathemas, and the Inquisitor stood beside him crying out the responses in his high harsh voice. As each batch was dealt with, it was handed over to the representatives of the secular arm and hustled off to its appointed stakes.

The last one was very special and made his own separate entrance, closely guarded. He was tied on a donkey, seated backwards, and his hat was taller and his robes gaudier than the rest. His pink eyes glared wildly in the blank pallor of his face, and his grin was more terrible than wrath. Even the pikemen stirred and muttered, and the crowd shrank back as he passed around the square: "Pink-eyes—pink-eyes—he has the very face of the evil one."

Cardinal Kraag looked down on him with a grim smile on his vast battered face.

"The sometime Lord William, for manifold sorceries and blasphemies beyond counting . . ."

The formula of excommunication droned on.

" . . . We deliver him now to the secular arm, adjuring them to use mercy towards him," concluded the Cardinal with satisfaction.

The albino was dragged from the donkey and carried to the tallest of the stakes. The one-eyed chief executioner gave the signal to his assistants who moved briskly forward, piling the faggots and blowing up the torches. Pink eyes blazing with rage and fear, Merganser yelled across the square.

"I invented this game, holy man, and my will is more nimble than yours. Remember the tower! remember the tower!"

The flickering of the Troublemaker intensified, and the scene of stakes and cowled figures cross-faded with another.

Amid the thunder of kettledrums, the tumbrils rolled into the Square of the Republic; the crowd roared out revolutionary songs, and red bonnets were tossed into the air. From the balcony of the Town Hall, Citizen Kraag, wearing over his uniform a red sash of office, raised his massive head and glowered down on the Square. It had been a near thing, he reflected, fingering the thickness of his bull neck; if he had not carried the Assembly with him last night . . . The first victim was being led up the steps to the lofty scaffold in the middle of the square; the little figures about the tall machine went about their business, and the triangular blade flashed in the sun. "One," shrieked the mob " . . . Two . . . Three . . ."

At each pause, the albino executioner strutted and postured across the front of the platform, a handsome figure in his fine uniform, with a red rose tucked behind his ear. He winked at the rows of girls who sat knitting at the foot of the scaffold, and they waved to him.

As the last waggon rolled into the square, the yells of the crowd drowned out the rumble of the kettledrums and the soldiers fitted bayonets and closed ranks about the scaffold. The assistants hustled him up the steps—the lean wizened figure of the Incorruptible, his linen foul, his face stubbled, glaring madly about him from his one good eye, the other having been destroyed by powder-burns in the scuffle when he was arrested.

They slammed him down brutally, face upwards, and strapped him to the plank. The elegant executioner leaned down and murmured: "One good turn deserves another, little old friend;" and the blade began to fall with the sound of an enormous steel kiss.

Inventing desperately, Paradine dissolved the square into a rapid stutter of montage. He swept down on his tormentors in a flurry of cavalry; but Merganser's infantry squares held firm, while Kraag played upon them both impartially with his massed artillery. Amid the thickening mirages, phantasmal armies of scarlet and blue, of blue and grey, of grey and khaki, attacked and counterattacked in mad confusion.

The battlefield spread out into a vast stretch of cratered mud and rolling clouds of smoke lit by lurid flares, in which Kraag, Paradine and Merganser staggered about, exhausted and bewildered, buffeted by their own creations. They sat down at last together on the edge of an abandoned trench, gasping and choking in the foul acrid air.

"Quits," sputtered Merganser.

"Pax," wheezed Paradine.

Kraag said nothing, but lumbered to his feet and towered over them.

"Now it is my turn," he growled. "You will find my dream large enough for you both."

The scene of the battlefield rippled like water, and resolved itself into a large room of marble pillars and red velvet draperies.

"I warn you, my patience is at an end." Chancellor Kraag stamped heavily up and down the ornate room, the parquet creaking beneath his polished jackboots. "For a month there have been reports from all over the country of this woman going about quite openly and holding some sort of religious services. Wherever she has appeared, there has been trouble. Yet your people haven't been able to do a thing about it. Perhaps it's time I got a new Minister of Security."

Paradine, from where he stood by one of the tall windows, turned his seamed parchment face towards Kraag.

"I think we may have what you want now, Chancellor," he said softly. Kraag tramped across the room and stood beside him, looking down into the square. Another rain squall slashed down across the bleak buildings, and the gate was being opened in the barbed-wire barricade, and one of the black police-cars drove in, to be immediately surrounded by guards.

A woman was bundled out into the rain, and even as she stood there in her shabby coat, she had a golden look, staring serenely at the guards with their tommy-guns pointing at her.

"Who is she working for?" said Kraag, as she was led up the steps.

Paradine shrugged. "Who knows? perhaps she's just a madwoman, no more. We'll soon find out."

"There's no time to lose," said Kraag, leading the way to the door. Paradine followed him, pausing to snap into the intercom: "We're on our way to room 101. Tell the chief interrogator to meet us there immediately."

The private lift took them down through the successive floors of gilt and plush and marble, into the deep basement, with its exposed concrete walls and naked lights. They marched in step down the echoing corridor, the gross bulky Chancellor and his shadowy dwarfish security chief, and the steel door at the end was opened to them.

The room was small and whitewashed, and contained an operating table, a stenographer's desk, and several cabinets of instruments. The woman stood quite still in the middle of the room, and rain ran out of her hair and down her old mackintosh and made a spreading puddle about her feet. She seemed gently indifferent, as if she expected them but did not care at all about them.

The white-haired interrogator turned from one of the cases and walked towards them. His black uniform with its silver lightning-flash badges was beautifully cut, and he dangled from his long white fingers a pair of glittering electrodes on wires, and hummed a gaily sentimental operatic tune.

"It is good to see a man who enjoys his work," growled the Chancellor.

"I have made a great discovery," said Merganser cheerfully. "All my life I have followed pleasure; now at last I know that it ends in the house of pain. Pain is the dark shadow of pleasure, and without it pleasure could not stand in the sunlight. I assert my absolute right to pleasure through the deep and awful joy of degrading and destroying another."

The golden woman ignored him, and continued to stare tranquilly at Paradine.

"I told you long ago," she said, "that you were only a dream within a dream. Now my dream is ending, and yours with it. There is nothing but the dream."

The cellar shook as the building above it and all the grey city dissolved in the rain and came slopping down in tons of mud. Paradine felt his mind suddenly boil up, as if a hidden spring of deep water had been unsealed, washing away the whole wreckage of his life. With sudden energy, he snatched the dangling wires from Merganser's hand, whipped them around his throat and pulled tight. Pink eyes popping, Merganser caught at his wrists, trying in vain to loosen the stranglehold. They staggered and fell and rolled about the floor. With jerky movements like a clockwork toy, Merganser's hand went to his holster, pressed his gun against Paradine and emptied the magazine into his body. But the wiry arms tightened convulsively in death and they lay tumbled together, Merganser's face purple, his fine uniform drenched in Paradine's blood.

"The dream is nearly over," said the woman. "You do not need them anymore. Look, Boss Kraag."

She opened the door, and they were standing in the temple, looking down the steps into the green pool. Kraag's people, who had lived in the city, came straggling in forlornly from the desert

"There are your people, Boss Kraag," said the woman. "They are yours alone. There is no longer the dreamer to hold up your right hand, and the joymaker to hold up your left hand. You are alone with them. What have you got to say?"

Kraag thrust his great battered face towards them and held up his arms and shouted:

"My people. I am your leader and there is no other. There is no other, there never has been any other. I am your very selves, the heart of our nation, the conscience of our race. Your will is one with mine. I led you out of the desert, and made you a mighty people. When you were corrupted and wallowed in the sins of the body, I chastised you and gave you the holy state. When your minds were set on unearthly things, I compelled you to become the equal state. When you were drunk with freedom, I gave you the ordered state. Now all these are nothing, for strength comes out of the desert, and must in the end return to it again."

As he was speaking, tall towers of dust rose and fell in the desert, swelling into mirages, and taking the form of a mountain, blue and shadowy with distance, shimmering into heights of eternal ice.

"We are one people, and I am your embodied will. I will lead you up into the mountain, and blaze forth upon you in holiness and joy and wisdom. We shall dwell there forever. History is at an end; I am its fulfillment."

He drew on his mantle and took up his staff, walking through the midst of them, and they fell in behind him, men, women and children, and trekked off across the waste. The golden woman watched them, as they walked through waters and fed on dews from heaven. After a time, they were no more than a file of ants trudging through a burning silence over the foothills and up to the slopes of the mountain. And the mountain was itself Kraag, old stony face staring down across the centuries of dust. Thunder pealed around the stone figure, and cloud veiled it, towering up to heaven, glowing with deadly radiance.

Alone in the desert, the golden woman puffed out her cheeks and blew gently, causing the cloud to drift away in long tatters and floating spires, until there was nothing left but a pleasant landscape of low green hills and wooded valleys. Drawing down with her the bodies of Paradine and Merganser, she sank into the golden pool, which lay for a long time reflecting the bright world like the pupil of a great eye. Slowly the landscape drained away into its reflection in the still mere, until there was only the reflection and nothing more. Then the pool was troubled; concentric waves rippled and spread across it. There was no pool, only waves of light radiating out into darkness.

SEVEN

THE SURVEY SHIP came out of overdrive with a hyperphotic bang which sent concentric shock waves of prismatic light spinning out into the void, rapidly fading down into the red, and out. The alarms went off at once. Still groggy from the buffeting of reentry, Paradine painfully focused blurred eyes on the scope, where a huge pale sun bulked terribly large and near. Sweating, he reached for the overdrive shift, and flipped it across; the auxiliary drives screamed and died. There was only one thing for it; he swung the ship hard over, and gave it a burst on full power. As the brutal g-forces crunched him back against the contoured padding and he blacked out, he hoped his copilot had had the sense or luck to stay in his autobunk . . .

. . . something cold and pungent was in his mouth and nostrils. Through a red fog, he could see Merganser bending over him with a resuscitube. He tried to sit forward, and nearly blacked out again with cramp.

"Easy now, captain sir," came Merganser's voice through the shrill metallic ringing. "No haste, see? we've plenty time now, maybe too much. Breath deeply now, do yourself good."

He raised the resuscitube again, and as the cold vapour hit him, the red mist cleared, and ringing in the ears died away.

"What happened?" mumbled Paradine stupidly.

"He wants to know what happened," said Merganser mock-patiently. "I wake up with the clangers going, and then the ship goes onto full power and the autobunk closes in on me, and when things stop banging around I'm out here and you're dead and the starboard tubes are fried. I closed all down just before she blew. Now, what happened?"

Paradine looked miserably at the dead board. "The mass-detector must have failed," he said. "We came out of subspace right beside the star. The gravity jammed the overdrive. All I could do was pull straight out."

"We're out, and that's all." Merganser waved his hand over the board. "No drive. Nothing."

"No power at all?"

Merganser's fingers flicked over the switches; the ship stirred and creaked.

"There's power in the small laterals. If there's a planet, not too far, we might get close enough to eject."

Paradine reached forward painfully, switched on the scanner and sat back while it hummed and clicked, feeling out for the star's planetary system, calculating probabilities, ready to lock on with the slow pulse of the life-detector system.

"It may take time," he said.

Merganser slumped in the other control-chair. "I was having this dream," he said. "We had this fight somewhere. I killed you, or you killed me, I'm not sure."

He stared with his pink eyes at the scanner, and whistled a gay tune which neither of them knew. Paradine reached over for the resuscitube, and took another whiff from it. The dullness in his head began to clear; the despair remained. Then the tape began to click out from the scanner, and the albino stopped whistling.

"Oxygen planet ... one point one seven gee ... standard rotation ... abundant vegetation ... query traces animal life ..."

Merganser pounded his fist on his knee. "A natural, the only one in the book. And who can we tell? No one. Will they make a search, think?"

"We're spread so thin," said Paradine. "It might be ten years, it might be a thousand. I'll switch on the beacon before we ditch. Someone'll hear it someday."

He fed the tape into the autopilot, adjusted the lateral jets, and watched the scanner as the ship swung round and drifted slowly off on its new course. "It'll take weeks," he said. "I'll get some sleep. Then

131

we'd better start loading the pods with everything we can carry."

"It'll be good to use one of these things," said Merganser. He was standing among a litter of gear, testing the feel of the heavy hunting-carbine. "I hope those traces of animal life are large and edible."

Paradine sealed up another case of syrettes and stacked them with the medical stores. "I never liked killing things," he said. "I'm an ecologist, remember? Live things are my study."

"I like a machine that does a good job," said Merganser, checking the ammunition clips. "Down there, it may be eat or be eaten. And how much food can we pack—ninety days?"

"We may end up vegetarians," said Paradine.

"Nothing like protein on the hoof," said Merganser.

They swung in the two escape pods, and carefully packed the waiting stores into them. Though designed strictly for emergencies within planetfall, the one-man pods allowed space for a good deal more then emergency supplies; but Paradine sighed at the packages still left over on the deck. Merganser thoughtfully removed a food-pack from his pod, and replaced it with a rack of concussion-grenades.

"Time to go," said Paradine. "Strap in. I'll set the autos and follow you."

"Happy landings, mon capitaine."

The new planet was in the scanner now, green and hazy. Paradine set the automatics for a planetary orbit and for ejection at the optimum point. He talked a final entry onto the log, switched on the radio beacon, and wedged himself into the pod among the clutter of carefully-packed supplies. The cover slid shut, and the pod vibrated as it was swung out into the ejector tube.

There was a thud and heavy g-pressure, and the two pods were curving away towards entry, leaving the ship to circle in its solitary orbit, its systems closing down one by one until only the sun-powered beacon remained, sending out its thousand-year-unanswered call.

They made planetfall close together, in a wide shallow valley enclosed on three sides by dark green forests which stretched away into the distance. It seemed as good a place as any for a base; they used the drogue-chutes to build a roomy tent in the hollow among a natural circle of stones, near a spring. Outlying stands of timber seemed to be uniformly of the same kind, all straight and about seven metres tall, with a single thick tuft of branches at the top. Cut, topped and notched by the portable laser, they provided a ready supply of building logs; and the two men set to work to build a blockhouse and stockade. It was heavy work in the rather high gravity and in the unchanging warm stillness of the valley, under the unclouded greenish sun.

Dressed only in shorts and sunglasses, Merganser slapped at a large slow fly which settled on his pink skin and drank his sweat. He said irritably:

"What's the hurry to build this soddered thing anyway?"

"We've been through all that," said Paradine. "Look—we don't know what season it is, or which way the year's turning, but I'd say it's high summer and we could have a cold winter yet. And for all we know, there could be natural enemies."

"Haven't seen a thing except these soddered musical flies, and they're friendly enough."

"It's early days yet. We heard those noises in the forest."

"All the more reason for a scout around. So that's what I'll do."

"Wait till we've got the blockhouse up," said Paradine reasonably. "It's only a few days. Then we'll go together. I can't do this alone."

Merganser stared at him, shrugged and, picking up the loaded carbine, slouched off towards the nearest mass of trees. Paradine fought down his anger. Taking the bio-test case, he sat down near the spring and began to check out another batch of plant-samples: so far, he had found two edible ones, a root and a berry, both rather unappetising. He couldn't blame Merganser entirely; pilot-teams on the Survey Mission were chosen for complementary qualities. It was bad luck that the cynical nerve and skill which made the albino valuable in space turned, on the ground, into an atavistic urge to wander and to hunt.

The crack of Merganser's carbine sounded quite close, and something came thrashing through the trees. A white thing came out into the clearing, man-high, dancing and skittering on its four long brittle-looking white legs. It teetered frantically about, panting and whistling, the big head and huge, mournful eyes turning this way and that in a terrified search for safety. Paradine stood up; the creature teetered over to him and went down, kneeling on all fours in front of him, with its sad eyes fixed on him beseechingly. There was a splash of red on its white woolly side.

With a crackling of branches, Merganser emerged on the edge of the wood, carbine at the ready. The beast gave a low sad cry, like a stricken man, and, scrambling to its feet, it began to totter agitatedly away from the spring. The carbine cracked again; the big head splattered, and the beast went down in a tangle of writhing limbs. Merganser came up, and they stared at it together.

"It attacked you, I suppose?" said Paradine bitterly.

"Not a bit. Friendliest critter I've ever seen."

"It was after something—help maybe. For all we know it's got intelligence."

"It was browsing," said Merganser. "You ought to know, mi capitano—the browsers never have time to develop intelligence. Just look at the sheen on the pelt, it's almost iridescent. Help me get it off, will you?"

They hoisted the body up on a triangle of poles, and carefully stripped off the white pelt before butchering the carcass. Paradine worked in glum silence; Merganser, as he worked, whistled the new tune between his teeth. The meat tested out edible. While Paradine started up the solid-fuel cooker and set some of the meat to stew with herbs and roots that he had found, the albino carefully scraped the pelt and stretched it out on the poles to dry in the sun.

"Extraordinary structure," he said as he came back from cleaning himself at the spring, "under the skin there's a sort of reticulation of sinewy stuff, and very slight muscle. That's how it could be so spindly."

"It was pretty ill-coordinated. I'd say there can't be much in the way of predators about."

"There are now, herr hauptmann," said Merganser cheerfully, taking another spoonful of his stew. "It cooks out really well. My compliments to the chef, of course."

Paradine managed a sour smile, then: "Listen," he said.

They could hear a faint mournful music, like the wandering vibration of a bass string.

"It's the pelt," said Paradine. "Look." They hurried over to it.

The pelt was shrinking and tightening rapidly as it dried, bending the poles inward. A light breeze blew across and struck the vibration from it; at the same time the iridescent sheen of the short white fur intensified, until waves of delicate prismatic colours swept across it. Suddenly all changed; the colours disappeared into a muddy brown, the pelt softened and sagged and stank.

In the next few weeks they completed the blockhouse but left the stockade unfinished. The weather was definitely cooler and solar measurements showed that the planet's year was a short one. Merganser hunted regularly and brought several more of the white creatures, which appeared to be solitary but fairly numerous, also a number of other things, including a fat-bodied flightless bird, several large rodents, and an amphibious creature whose flavour suggested the presence of fish.

As the sun swept lower day by day, they decided to make one trek before winter closed in, in the direction of what appeared to be a break in the forest far off on the slope of the horizon. It was easy going among the straight regular trees, along level swards and gentle slopes, treading through low friable undergrowth which was already dry and ready to powder beneath their feet. There were streams and marshy places, but no large waters to cross.

Merganser hunted as they went, and although they found only the same timid game, they kept watches at night. It was on the third night, while Paradine was dreaming confusedly of tall incredible buildings towering up terrace by terrace from a calm starlit sea, that he was jolted suddenly awake by the sound of Merganser's carbine. It cracked again.

"What is it?" said Paradine in a low voice.

"Over there. Green eyes in the dark. Up a tree, I'd say."

"Night vision. That usually means a predator. It might be a bird that goes after the small stuff."

In the morning they searched and found no tracks; but Paradine thoughtfully examined one of the trees where ribbons of bark had been ripped and hung down. The trees were very close together here, and the tufted branches at the top formed a natural platform, on which an agile creature could have moved a long way without touching ground.

About noon, the trees began to thin out as they approached the clearing. Merganser was in the lead when they came to a final break in the trees; he pointed silently out into the greenish sunlight, towards a low dark shape. Unmistakable even at the distance, it was a squat tower built of rough stone blocks.

As Paradine hurried up beside him, there was a sudden spang and a whurr; a sprung tree jerked up, drawing a net about them. The carbine went flying, and they were tumbled helplessly together and jerked up into the air.

There was a quick movement below. Looking down, Paradine saw what seemed to be a little furry man who darted from the trees and stared up at them with anxious whiskered face. He quickly raised a long tube to his mouth and blew. Merganser cried out and tried to reach his leg.

"The soddered thing," he shrieked, "it's poisoned—" His body went limp. Another little furry man darted

136

out from the other side, and raised his pipe. Paradine felt a sharp pain in his arm, and saw a long black thorn stabbed in through the sleeve. Then the tower and the clearing and the furry men swam away into darkness.

He was dreaming again of the tall terraces towering above the sea. They were empty and silent now, the halls and galleries strewn with rubbish, the sound outside of guns or thunder, the war still going on. His mouth and throat burned with a consuming thirst. When he leaned down to drink from the basin of the fountain, it filled with fine dry sand, which overflowed and spread everywhere with a faint silken hissing. As the tide of sand overbore him and swept him along, he scrabbled desperately about and grasped the carved shape of a tactile, old and worn very smooth, so that his fingers struck from it only the faintest of vibrations. The light shook and shimmered, becoming tower, desert, cathedral, factory, abandoned café, space cruiser, battlefield. The warrior stooped over him, blackness behind the eyeholes of the steel mask, and drove downwards with a blade that spun and blurred into mist as it sliced down his left side leaving a wake of intolerable pain. A scream tore from his parched throat and he awoke to—
—bright light, and a bewhiskered little man looking down at him with sad eyes, and the pain real. The little man said something in a rough voice, other faces bobbed about, and a sharp pain in his right arm brought back the dark.

When he woke again, slowly, he was lying down on a bed, in a pale uncertain light which might have been dawn. The pain had gone, but a numbness and tingling had taken its place. For a time he simply lay there, trying to adjust and regain control. Someone was snoring at his left, and turning there, he found Merganser's head lying very close, almost touching his own. The albino's face was white and puffy, with shadowed eyes and a pale growth of beard. They must have both been under for quite a long time.

137

The sleeping face repelled him, and he drew away. The face followed, and remained almost touching his. He tried to turn on his side, and Merganser's head lifted and flopped, and his weight seemed to be holding Paradine down. The snoring choked off: Merganser's pink eyes bleared open. They were both struggling to sit up, and staring down unbelievingly at their body. Up to about the waist it was Paradine's body, known to him by all its familiar landmarks; but the trunk had been extensively reconstructed: Paradine's left arm, shoulder and side seemed to have been cut away, and Merganser's left section, complete with head, grafted on. A thick pink welted scar marked the join.

The Merganser head leaned back and began to laugh shrilly and uncontrollably. The Paradine head turned aside and retched. For a few minutes the composite body writhed and rolled off the bed and threshed about like drunken men wrestling, as impossible demands were made on the enlarged but shared lungs and stomach.

"Control—breathing," choked the Paradine head, setting his teeth hard to master the vomit. They sat together, their joint body sweating, eyes closed, as they fought back for breath.

"Speak short sentences," said Paradine. "On the outbreath. Mustn't happen again. Could choke to death."

"Holy sweet Nobodaddy," said Merganser, looking down at their body. He began to laugh again.

"Stop," said Paradine sharply, "it." He was getting hiccups.

"It—I mean us—it's mostly you. But what have they *done*?"

Paradine was carefully touching their chest with his fingers. "It's the two heads," he said. "That must be it. The rest is ancillary. There's a double heart-beat, I think. Additional lung capacity. Common digestive system. I wonder how we are for locomotor system?"

They eased themselves gently off the bed, tried to move both legs together, and tumbled over onto the stone floor. Scrambling up, they stood poised, and

138

Paradine said: "We'll have to do it by numbers. You step off slowly now—left—right—left—right ..." Like a pair of spastics running a three-legged race, they moved slowly around the dim circular room, Paradine spreading out his right hand to touch the rough stone wall.

The thick wooden door creaked open, and one of the little hairy men came in pushing a trolley. With gruff, reassuring noises, he motioned them to sit on the bed, and uncovered two earthware pots of savoury stew. While they began to eat with wooden spoons, the hairy man stood watching them, and they watched him. He stood over a metre high, with short bandy legs and a long body, narrow shoulders, deep chest, stubby hands with black finger nails. Except for a sort of leather sporran across the loins, his body was covered by a thick coat of greyish hair, which also thickly thatched his head. His eyes had the familiar mournful look, and beneath dark nostrils, his mouth was hidden behind a sweeping moustache.

He watched them eating with evident anxiety and pleasure. When they had quite finished, he pointed to himself and said distinctly: "Tagmaun."

They repeated the word.

He pointed to them and said, with a note of enquiry: "Boscumin?"

Paradine nodded and repeated: "Boscumin."

The Tagmaun gave a little skip of pleasure. Then he wheeled the trolley away, pausing in the doorway to bow very low, until his whiskers touched the ground.

"Whatever we are, we're special," said Merganser. "I wonder what boscumin means? Stranger? Friend? Freak?"

"It's something they've got a name for," said Paradine. "We've been rebuilt to a pattern. And it's something they respect."

They lay back carefully together and stared up at the ceiling of the beehive-shaped room, where a circular skylight let in the fading greenish sunshine. Merganser giggled: "I wonder if they've got liquor? If I get sloshed, admiral, we'll both have the hangover."

A few days later, the first Tagmaun, who seemed to be some kind of attendant, brought with him a second, quite different in character. He was nearly a head taller, and his coat, which had been a rich chestnut, was streaked with white. He was evidently to be their teacher, and the little attendant paid deference to him. But they noticed that he remained standing throughout the lesson, and when the two Tagmauni withdrew, they both made obeisance, though the teacher had to be helped to his feet again afterwards.

The language was so simple and easily mastered that within a few weeks they could speak it with reasonable fluency; and one morning Paradine said to the teacher:

"Why have you brought us here? Why has this been done to us?" He drew his finger down the long welted scar that joined their bodies.

The teacher's brown eyes shifted uneasily from side to side. "It was the will of the Wise and Mighty One" (he used the singular noun Boscumin).

"But you call us the Wise and Mighty One," said Merganser.

The teacher began to back slowly towards the door.

"The words of the Wise and Mighty One are full of meaning, hard to understand," he said, bowing shakily to the floor.

When the attendant came alone, bringing their evening meal of bread sopped in marrow-soup, Paradine asked him again:

"Why are we here? Why was this done?"

The little Tagmaun started back, his grey whiskers quivering. "The Wise One knows," he said excitedly, "the Wise One knows. He came through the sky. He came in a great ring of light. He was broken apart in the fall. We found him. The wise men put him together. Now we have a god again." He leaped about the room, giving excited cries, and rushed up to kiss their hands and feet; then, suddenly abashed, he withdrew from the room, bowing several times.

"So we've come back," said Merganser.

"I thought it must be something like that," said Paradine. "This must be a derivative culture. They've retained something, highly sophisticated surgery, perhaps other things as well. In other ways, they've regressed to the primitive. But the people who really developed the advanced culture must have gone away. It's always the same. The gods made it: they went away. Someday they will come back."

"It's their tough luck when they do," said Merganser.

They lay back on the bed, with its coverings of silky furs, and stared up at the darkening sky. Although they had worked out between them a reasonable way of living, sleeping was still a discomfort, since they could lie only on their back. Merganser snored: Paradine talked in his sleep.

The round, featureless stone room was becoming unspeakably tedious to them. Survey-teams were chosen for complementary qualities and compatibility, but not at such close quarters as this, when complementaries broke down into mere opposites within the confines of a single body. When Merganser wanted to sleep, Paradine might be intensely awake, stirring restlessly on the couch; when Paradine wished to meditate, Merganser might prefer to pace irritably about the room; when Paradine, lacking appetite, pushed aside his stew, Merganser would finish it off and give both indigestion. Sharing one body was almost a sharing of minds, and when Merganser raged in their prison, as he often did, Paradine's brain felt giddy with the sudden flood of adrenalin. They no longer spoke to each other, except for physical necessities, and looked forward to the teacher's daily visit, and to the crudely-printed picture books he now brought them, as a distraction.

At last, one day, he asked very deferentially whether the Wise and Mighty One would consent to appear to his people, and they agreed with relief.

Early next morning, the old, russet-coloured teacher and the little grey attendant ushered in two more Tagmauni. One was large old and fat but of great

141

dignity, with the eyes and mouth drawn into the steep sagging lines of his venerable face. The other was thin, smooth, parti-coloured, with long sharp features. After formal obeisances of some complexity, they endued their god with a robe made from the fur of the white spindly animals. There was some difficulty in getting it over the heads, but it was beautifully warm and soft, and so treated as to retain its delicate polychrome iridescence.

The door was opened, and they were ushered out into light and a sudden hush of noise. They were vaguely aware that a semicircular wall, whitewashed and roughly pictured, enclosed them from behind; overhead was a steep conical roof which seemed to be made of a sort of open basketwork, for the sunlight filtered through it making pale-green spangles. In front was a semi-circle of wooden pillars and beyond, in the sunlight, what appeared to be an open sward, and a great crowd of the Tagmauni. Paradine and Merganser were now prepared for the physical variety of their captors: their height varied by nearly half a metre, the colour of their body-hair from pure white to glossy dark, their shape from slender to squat.

They watched in silent anxious adoration as their twi-headed god was led forward and seated in the centre of the circular enclosure on a massive throne of carved dark wood. Then they broke out into harsh sharp cries, and milled about. Little groups, breaking away, ran forward eagerly, and ceremoniously made water in the stone runnels at the foot of the pillars. When all had thus paid their respects, they sat down quietly on the grass, waiting expectantly. Paradine turned his head towards Merganser's, and nodded in the direction of one of the wall-paintings. Drawn in crude colours, it showed an immense two-headed creature leading two small Tagmauni, who seemed to be trotting on all fours, on some kind of leash. On the opposite wall was a similar picture, except that the Boscumin in this case was obviously female.

"There's your old civilisation," said Paradine.

"And what are these?" said Merganser. "Escaped pets, perhaps?"

"Just that."

The old Tagmaun stepped forward, and said in his deep old voice:

"Will the Wise and Mighty Ones graciously answer the questions?"

Merganser's pink eyes flickered towards Paradine, who answered: "Yes."

The old one cleared his throat, and holding up a sheet of yellowed parchment, read the first question: "What is truth?"

"Truth is one and indivisible," said Paradine.

"Truth is that which most contradicts itself," said Merganser.

"What is the relation between the One and the Many?"

"The Many are the broken reflections of the One," said Paradine.

"The One is a phantom abstraction of the Many," said Merganser.

"What is the nature of the Universe?"

"A creative act maintained by miracle," said Paradine.

"A material flux maintained by chance," said Merganser.

"What is the law of existence?"

"Necessity is the acceptance of freedom," said Paradine.

"Freedom is the acceptance of necessity," said Merganser.

"What is the purpose of life?"

"Self-forgetting—" said Paradine.

"Self-fulfilment—" said Merganser.

"—knowledge—"

"—pleasure—"

"—wisdom—dedication—peace—" said Paradine.

"—joy—power—grandeur—" said Merganser.

"What are your secret names?"

"Night," said the dark head of Paradine.

"Day," said the white head of Merganser.

The old one bowed to the floor, and the young one turned to the multitude and said: "They have heard the questions, they have given the answers. The two-fold wisdom has returned to live with us."

The Tagmauni began to leap about with sharp cries, and the whole assembly rapidly turned into an orgy. Their sexual customs proved to be somewhat embarrassing.

The sessions in the open temple were repeated every few days, but without the celebration. Although crowds of spectators came to watch, the real participants came singly or in small groups. While others waited patiently, the petitioners or disputants would nervously make water by the pillars, before being led forward, usually by the sharp-featured young Tagmaun, who directed the ceremony and glossed or interpreted the oracle. They were called upon to decide various practical matters such as the division of property, the allocation of children, the fidelity of mates or the settlement of feuds. Since they invariably gave contradictory answers, to which the young Tagmaun gave his own interpretation, everyone was satisfied and honoured their collective wisdom.

Thus, two dishevelled young females were brought before them; they had been scuffling over a youngling, which one claimed as natural mother, the other as foster-nurse.

"Let the natural mother have it," said Paradine. "No tie is stronger than the blood."

"Let the foster mother have it," said Merganser, "otherwise you'll upset the child."

"Now hear the words of the Wise and Mighty One," said their sharp-faced interpreter, "let each mother keep the child for half a year in turn."

There was polite applause.

Or a powerful, grey-whiskered Tagmaun, his hide striped with old scars, was dragged before them; he had commanded a levy in a hard-fought skirmish with the Tugherim, and when his own son had run from the battlefield, he had struck him down.

"Let him be rewarded for putting duty to the state above personal affection," said Paradine.

"Let him be driven out for breaking the bonds of kinship," said Merganser.

"Hear the wisdom," said the interpreter; "he shall be rewarded and driven out into the forest."

The audience went away arguing.

Winter came soon, and for a time there were no more gatherings. Snow fell thickly, and flashed into emerald lights in the glow of the greenish sun. Thick fur robes were brought for them; the stone room was warmed with charcoal heaters, and lit by small oil lamps set in brackets, for the snow blanked out the skylight. After they had exhausted every topic of conversation, they sank into a bored and savage silence, pacing round and round the room or lying on the couch, staring upwards.

Then one day when new sunlight streamed in through the skylight and the open door, they were robed and led out again into the circle of the temple. The crowd was a very large one, the multi-coloured heads stretching away to where the forest showed a wall of new green. In front of the temple, guarded by heavy black Tagmauni, was something tall and square, hidden by fur drapes.

The old Tagmaun whom they now called the Bishop came forward, the immense wrinkles of his face more bowed and slanted by age; his sharp-faced young assistant, the Deacon, was beside him. After the usual ceremonies, the Bishop asked: "Wise and Mighty Ones, a question. Is it right to make war?"

"War is the greatest of all evils," said Paradine promptly.

"War is the fulfilment of our natural impulses," said Merganser at the same time.

"Hear the wisdom," shouted the Deacon, "war is evil unless it is fought in self-defence."

There was a great commotion of shouting, leaping and water-making, which turned into hysteria when the covering was dragged away, revealing a cage. Something quick brown and angry moved about inside, and hissed.

"We offer you the spring sacrifice," shouted the Deacon, "a warrior of the Tugherim."

145

"Tugher! Tugher! Tugher!" shouted the frenzied crowd.

The front of the cage swung open and the black guards dragged forward the Tugher in his chains. He was, by Tagmaun standards, of middle height, and like them he was bow-legged and long-bodied, but where most of the Tagmauni seemed strong and clumsy, this creature was swift and lithe, with powerful flat muscles straining under his ginger fur. He had a flat fanged pointed head, that swung this way and that like a snake's, and as he was dragged into the temple, his eyes glinted green in the gloom.

"Those eyes," muttered Merganser, "it's the night-hunter."

Dragged and in chains, the Tugher still looked about him with fathomless contempt and pride. In a high nasal voice he cried out:

"I claim the warrior-captive's right of last words."

"Speak."

"This then. Ffssst." His head shot forward and he spat with great accuracy in the face of the old Bishop. With a sinewy spring, he dragged himself free and began to flail away with his loose chains at the black guards.

Several went down, and the rest crouched away, trying to cover themselves and at the same time to form a human shield in front of their twi-headed god. A great howling and shouting went up from the mob, who edged and darted closer, not yet daring to get within range of those murderous flails. For a long moment the Tugher stood at bay on the temple steps, turning slowly about, fierce and splendid, his furry body bristling with rage. Then a fresh squad of guards burst in, and the Tugher with a shriek began to claw his way up one of the wooden pillars of the Temple. The Tagmauni crowded in with a rush, and a wave of bodies swept up and over the Tugher and plucked him to the ground. There was a great screaming and worrying and a struggling mass of bodies, out of which the sharp-faced Deacon suddenly uprose waving a long red knife. The broken body was tossed up, to be dragged and tumbled by the mob out in the open.

"He was brave—" said Paradine.

"—but a fool," said Merganser.

"A savage."

"They're all savages."

Paradine put his hand over his eyes; Merganser craned forward to see the end.

When it was over, the mob quietened and the Deacon came forward, his robes torn and stained.

"One more question, Wise and Mighty One. You have now seen the Tugherim—they are vermin. Is it just that we attack them?"

"No," said Paradine.

"Yes," said Merganser.

"Hear the wisdom," shouted the Deacon, "it is right for us to attack them in self-defence, before they are able to attack us."

The Wise and Mighty One struggled to its feet. "No," said Paradine loudly, "don't listen to him. Everything he says is twisted to his own meaning. We are not gods—"

"Quiet, you fool," said Merganser, "do you want us to go the same way?"

"Anything would be better—"

Somewhere in the middle of the crowd a bright flash lit the dusk and there was a heavy vibrating explosion; Tagmauni were sent flying, or staggered about, clutching their heads. Looking upwards, they caught a glimpse of something outlined against the green evening sky, something like a huge kite, with a Tugher held to it underneath by body-straps. It flashed across the clearing and disappeared into the forest. Another sailed over, and there was a second explosion.

Merganser began to laugh softly. "The Tugher had the same idea. And they've got flight."

"They've raided the blockhouse and found your concussion-grenades," said Paradine. "A near hit from one of those things can homogenize you."

More kite-gliders flitted over, and more grenades fell. The Tagmauni were mauling and trampling over

147

one another to get away, but there was already a
clamour of fighting on the edge of the woods. Forgetting their painfully learned co-ordination, Paradine
and Merganser stumbled and crawled back into the
bed-chamber, closed the massive door and leaned
against it, choking for breath.

"We shouldn't have let it get to this," said Paradine.
"If only you'd left it alone."

"If only you'd left it alone," said Merganser in the
same breath.

"You and your silly-clever answers—"

"You soddering old preacher—Great Nobodaddy,
how I hate you."

Merganser's hand, the left one, suddenly swung up
and clawed at Paradine's throat. With the blood and
breath strangled out of Paradine, Merganser was getting a double ration, and he tightened his grip with
manic strength. Swimming in a red haze, Paradine
swung his fist into their joint solar plexus, and they
doubled up groaning on the floor. Merganser's thumb
came up gouging, but Paradine's hand, the right one,
caught him by the wrist, and they hand-wrestled,
grunting and rolling about the floor of the darkening
room. Their body poured sweat. The hands slipped.
With a huge effort, Merganser clasped the heavy
table and pulled them up, feeling for a knife he knew
to be there. Paradine's hand thumped against the side
of his pale head and pushed; Merganser's hand
swung up, pushing against the other dark head; they
stood in the middle of the floor, locked and straining
apart, whimpering with the effort.

Glass shattered and tinkled about them. Straining,
looking stupidly up with their two faces, they saw a
great star of evening sky smashed in the glass of the
skylight, framing the fierce flat head of a Tugher
peering down at them. Something small and black
pitched down. There was a blinding flash and a
booming explosion, and rings of huge sonic pressure
which spread and rebounded from the circular walls,
pulverizing all within, and an intolerable wrenching.
A jagged split drove through the centre of the raging
sound, making all fall apart.

148

EIGHT

THERE HAD BEEN an accident. He remembered, the laboring ship, the tilting, the fall. Out in the nothing, they had had an accident. Billy Merganser opened his eyes, dazzled by the light, and tried weakly to raise his head. An immense impalpable burden seemed to weight down his legs and all the right side of his body; but his left hand felt free. Leaning his head to the left, he looked and felt about. He seemed to be lying on an operating table, his body swathed in some kind of bulky surgical covering, from under which tubes filled with coloured fluids ran to a pulsing glittering machine.

He closed his eyes with a feeling of sick relief. They had been found in time, or at least he had; there would be time to think of the others later. He was out of it; a rescue-scoop must have reached him in time. Now that the robot-medics had him in hand, they could repair the damage, no matter what it might be. He was safe. But as disturbing after-images focused in his mind, he opened his eyes again.

The operating table and the glittering machine were standing in the middle of an immense purple plain. As far as he could tell with his limited field of vision, they were all alone on the sad flat plain, which stretched away on every side to a sharp horizon of magenta hills, while a featureless unchanging orange sky stretched overhead.

A tall inhuman figure moved across his field of sight, like an enormous mantis, its body covered in green laquered mail, moving upright with many-jointed limbs. It delicately reached out a serrated fore-limb and touched a switch on the glittering machine.

Something moved beside him and a second figure came into view, towering over him. The head, with its immense faceted eyes and cruel mandibular jaws,

149

was silhouetted against the orange light. He closed his eyes quickly, and two voices began speaking inside his head. One said:

"The shock reaction is deepening, master. I've increased the concentration."

"Can it take much more?"

"Very little. We can't maintain much longer."

"A pity. It's a very strange metabolism, and we shan't learn much more about it once it ceases to function. It's badly damaged; there must be quite a lot missing."

"Even if we understood it, master, we could never manufacture the spare parts in time."

"Of course, one could make some pretty good guesses on general morphological principles. Look."

Merganser could feel the surgical covers being lifted, but kept his eyes tightly shut.

"The undamaged upper node which contains sense organs is undoubtedly symmetrical, and as I have often taught you, nearly all life forms follow the rule of symmetry. The exceptions are few, though puzzling. Now you will notice that it has a limb. For what purpose, would you say?" Something hard and dry touched Merganser's left hand.

"For locomotion?"

"Unlikely. That delicately splayed extremity is undoubtedly prehensile and manipulative. No, we have to assume at least two further pairs of limbs for locomotion."

"Would not one pair be sufficient, master?"

"An interesting hypothesis, but unlikely. Maintaining balance would be enormously difficult, you see."

"Yes, master."

"Now here are traces of a respiratory system, it's hard to say what. And then one would have to postulate digestive and reproductive systems, and so on. I'm afraid we've really very little to go on."

"Is it intelligent, master?"

"What would you say?"

The light dry touch moved over his forehead and his closed eyelids.

"From the ingenious but limited external sense organs, I should guess that it is of a low order."

"Yet the contacts we have made with its mind are sharp and varied, though extremely confused. Very interesting, very puzzling. Much of it is surely delirium, but it's hard to say how much."

There was silence, in which the machine pulsed on.

"Where did it come from, do you think, master?"

"From somewhere up there, like the other unexplained objects that turn up from time to time. If only it weren't for the opacity. This is an unsatisfactory place to live in."

"It's the only place we have, master."

Another silence, and the pulsing grew faster.

"It's on maximum now, master, and I think perhaps it is becoming aware. Is there anything else?"

"We can give it comfort in its death. In the end, what more can one do?"

Merganser's eyelids fluttered open, and he caught a last glimpse of the sad purple plain and the crepuscular orange sky, and the two armoured heads staring down at him with their great inhuman eyes.

He thought that the light dry touch on his forehead and eyelids was repeated, and remained. Then he thought that the master was saying to him: "I show you the pictures in your mind. Tell me when to stop." He thought that the pictures glided across, one after the other, like projections on a solido screen. He saw Paradine, who could have been his friend; he saw himself as Helena's lover, in a various strange rooms; he saw boardrooms and staterooms and tall hotels and the unendurable radiance of deep space; he saw triumphant tournaments and the crumbling faces of frightened men, bedrooms, yoshiwaras, backalleys. None of them satisfied him, as they flickered by, more and more slowly. At last, there was only a street of broken pavements and garbage and peeling walls, which seemed to go on for ever, and he felt bitter defeat and the sadness in the mind of the master. But at the end of the street was a river which flashed into ruddy gold, and he knew it as he ran down the bank towards it, tearing off his dirty fine clothes.

Something mercifully released him as he plunged into the rapids of the cool water, which carried him on between the tall banks and out into the broad shallows. There were fish in the water, pale yellow as platinum, and when he put his head under the water he could hear them chirruping. There were deep sheltering trees above the far bank, and beneath them sitting on the grass, as he knew she would be, was the old woman. He ran up out of the river, splashing the golden water with his short fat legs, and nestled down beside her. She smelt like summer grass. She put her arm around him and let down her long white hair, which was as bright as silver and as fine as thistledown. They sat there together, watching the changing splendours of the river, and presently he knew that she was singing him a slow song which mingled with the music of the water, until the two became one, and he slept.

NINE

AT FIRST HE was aware only of vague sensations, of the dim stars overhead, of the sound of moving water, of the thick salty smell of sea-things. Then, as his head cleared, Paradine realised that he was cradled in two vast hands, the skin of which was thick and wrinkled and cold, growing out as webbing between the huge fingers, so that the cupped hands held him as in an enormous shell. He was being held clear of the water; the foam dashed along below. He knew what to expect, for he had seen them before, he thought, if only at a distance, the seagiants, descendants of a race who had taken to the waters many ages before, and had adapted to the life of sea mammals and grown vastly in bulk in the weightless conditions of the sea. Turning his head he could see the tall face behind him, with the foam breaking against the wide mouth and the flat slitted nostrils formed for closure under the water. Beneath the low forehead and bristling hair, the small eyes stared down at him vacuously. They were a simple and kindly people, with small intelligence.

Paradine tried to raise himself and fell back almost fainting. A compress of sea plants had been bound against the frightful wound in his left side; it seemed to have stopped the bleeding but not the pain, and he felt weak and cold.

Lifting his great head a little, the seagiant snorted; a rank ocean-smell breathed across Paradine. "Lie thtill," said the seagiant, in a booming indistinct voice like the humming of deep waters, "mutht wetht, poor mathter vewy thick, bad wound, vewy bad, lie thtill, take mathter to fwiend, kind, good, fwiend heal wound, mutht wetht, twutht theaman."

When Paradine lay back in the cup of the enormous clammy hands, everything went vague again, except the dim stars and the rushing waves.

153

A long time later, the stars had changed, he seemed to hear a distant shout across the dark water. The seagiant heard it too and halted, floating gently in the water, while the great head with its tiny flap-protected ears turned slowly about, trying to get a bearing on the sound. It came again. The seagiant boomed in reply, and set off in a smooth effortless rush. Peering between the giant hands, Paradine could see a light that bobbed and flickered and drew rapidly closer across the dark rolling waters. The dizzyness came and he leaned his head against the cold webbed fingers.

When he could look again, he was already being raised against the curved wooden side of a ship. A man in rough seafarer's clothes was holding a lantern and staring down at him. The seagiant rested one hand on the ship's rail, while with the other he gently transferred Paradine to a litter on the deck. The man saluted with his hand, and said: "Thank you, seagoer, once more I am in your debt."

"For nothing," rumbled the seagiant. "You thaved my thon, after the deep fishing. I go."

"Go well, then."

The man raised the lantern and bent over Paradine. As he did so, the thick lock of grey hair which covered his left eye tossed aside, and Paradine could see that there was no eye, only the cleft scar of a deep sword-cut which had slashed right across brow and cheek.

"So you're back again," he said softly, "and not before time either. It always comes to this."

"Who are you?" whispered Paradine.

"Don't you know?"

"No."

"Perhaps it's just as well. It would be terrible to know. Now drink this and be still. I've work to do and there's so little time, there's never enough time."

Paradine felt his head raised and a cup of something that tasted like mulled wine held to his lips. He sank immediately into a warm sleep.

When he awoke, he thought at first that only a

brief time had passed, for it was still night. But the moon had rounded out from dark to bright, and feeling down his left side, he was astonished to find that there was no sign of the terrible jagged wound, and his left arm flexed as firmly as his right. He sat up on the litter, the covers falling away, and looked down at his healed body.

The tall man was leaning against the mast, his one eye gleaming as he stared up at the moon.

"So," he said, turning to Paradine, "all begins again."

"I owe you my life," said Paradine, "who are you?"

"You may call me the Gespenster, though that is a function rather than a name. People call me all sorts of things—spy, healer, fighter, magician. I am all of these, and more, and none."

He pulled over a folding stool and sat down beside the litter. The ship sailed soundlessly on; they seemed to be the only two aboard, yet the sail was trimmed and the ship kept her course, and Paradine seemed to see shadows moving here and there, out of the corners of his eyes.

"What can you remember?" asked the Gespenster.

Paradine felt bewildered; he had a sense of identity and of a past, yet it was all formless and the details eluded him.

"I remember—what?—journeys and achievements and struggles but—" he touched his forehead—"they are no longer there."

"Good. The past is gone, now we must think of your future. What do you wish to be? a builder, warrior, trader, traveller, learned man? a King perhaps?"

"I think I could be a King."

"Good, again, but there are certain difficulties in your case. You can inherit a kingdom, of course, if you belong to the right family, or at least marry into one. But for a young landless man without family, like yourself, it is more difficult. The only really practical thing to do is to find a perilous princess, undergo the required ordeals and then marry her."

"Somewhere, I don't know how, I have suffered a

great defeat. I'm not sure that I should be found worthy."

"Wedding perilous princesses is a career like any other," said the Gespenster matter-of-factly, "and no more difficult for a man with the necessary aptitudes. I think I know just the right opening for you. Eat now and sleep, we haven't far to go." Beside the litter was a platter of bread and cheese and a flask of wine. The Gespenster leaned against the rail, staring out silently into the night with his one bright eye; the breeze stiffened in the sail and the ship altered course to starboard.

The city to which the Gespenster directed him was some distance inland from the coast, behind a range of hills covered with thick forests of oak and beech. His counsellor left him there, and he walked on alone down the road towards the city gate. Seen at a distance through the morning mist, the walls and gateworks of the city seemed imposing enough, but the closer he approached, the older and more dilapidated they seemed. The moat had spread out into a marsh, over which the road was carried on a roughly-cobbled causeway. The walls still towered up from their ancient base of massive cyclopean stones, but the upper parts showed plainly where gaps had fallen or been torn in the stonework, and repaired with stretches of brickwork, rubble or plain rough concrete. The great wooden gates, still showing scraps of bronze sheathing, sagged uselessly against the wall, and a single sentry, busily roasting a rabbit for his breakfast over a small fire, paid no attention to him.

Inside the walls, the single main street was weed-grown and wandered along with no set pattern. The low-squatted houses had the same kind of mean patchwork look; embedded in their walls he could see delicately fluted pillars, laid lengthwise and used as courses of masonry, broken gravestones, unidentifiable clunks of statuary, fragments of carved bas-reliefs and irregular pieces of mosaic, still glittering faintly under their glaze of grime. A few ragged people scuttered like vermin in and out of the doors of houses.

The same tatterdemalion architecture surrounded the central square, except where, on one side, rose the palace, or what was left of it. The outline of its elegance remained, not patched-up but simply peeling; here and there the morning sun struck motes of light from a gilded cupola or peacock-blue tile, but much of the surface, porcelain or stucco, had simply fallen away and lay as a scrap of rubbish around the base of the walls, leaving bare brick or lathe behind.

He stared at it, thinking contemptuously that the Gespenster was offering him a poor prospect. Then a bell sounded somewhere, and an old man in a stained tabard came out from the palace gate. He stood by the rubbish-choked fountain in the centre of the square, blew once on his trumpet, and said in a tired breathless voice: "Hear ye. All princes and men of good breeding. The princess offers her hand in marriage to anyone who will undertake three quests etcetera etcetera. Conditions can be had on application. Any applicant who fails or refuses will be fed to the palace dogs. Hear ye."

The old herald walked slowly back to the palace, and, as if in answer to his last statement, a hungry clamour of hounds sprang up inside. Paradine hesitated for a long moment, shrugged and followed the old man inside. He followed him down long dim corridors muffled in dust and cobwebs, into a tall room where the only light fell slanting from the clerestory windows high up under the roof. The beamed roof and panelled walls, once bright with honey coloured wood, were now sagging and mildewed. The hall was empty except for a highbacked chair on a dais at one end.

A door opened in the panelling and a girl stepped softly into the room. She was robed in some vague shadowy colour, moving like a sleepwalker across the dais towards the chair. When she turned, her blue eyes stared out blankly, not seeing him. The old herald muttered: "A claimant for the quest, your highness," and sat down wearily on the edge of the dais.

In a toneless voice, the princess began:

"Beyond the ice there is a bowl
The bowl is guarded by the beast
Slay the beast and bring the bowl.
The drowned city hides the sword
The sword is guarded by the man
Kill the man and bring the sword.
Beyond the mountains is the helm
The helm is guarded by the ghost
Lay the ghost and bring the helm."

Then she gabbled out like a child finishing a lesson:
"That's the quest and if you win you marry me and if
you don't you'll be eaten by the dogs." Somewhere
near, the voices of the hounds sounded hollowly.

There was a long silence. The princess stood unmoving in her faded robes, while the old herald
thoughtfully polished his trumpet on his sleeve. At
last Paradine said: "Is that all? can't you tell me more
about the quest?"

"Take it or leave it," said the princess in a cross,
childish voice. Paradine looked about the tall room
where the sunlight sloped down on ruined elegance.
"I'll take it," he said. With a sudden imperious gesture, the girl held out her right hand, and as he bent
forward and bowed to kiss it, she seemed to see him
for the first time. When the sound of his footsteps
padded away in the dust of the corridor, she slumped
into the high chair and wept helplessly.

Outside in the square, Paradine found the Gespenster waiting by the dry fountain with four shaggy
ponies, two saddled for riding and two already loaded with baggage. He told him the quest.

"It's not as hard as it sounds," said the Gespenster.
"Every child has heard the story of the Grey Bear
and the Bowl of Dream Water. I'll tell it to you as we
ride; there's no time to waste; we'll meet snow long
before we get there."

For some weeks they trekked northward across the
coastal plain. Snow came and went, and was begin-

ning to lie among the thin grass, where even the
hardy ponies could scarcely find enough grazing. Paradine did not think it strange to live in this winter
world, with its sky of perpetual overcast in which the
sun, when it appeared, was always low red and swollen, the old sun of an old world. Across the frozen
tundra they rode slowly towards the ice-blink in the
north, where age by age the edge of the ice-cap ate
its way across the plains.

Even so, it was almost a surprise to him when, one
morning, they came to the ice-wall which had
hovered for so many days on their horizon. The Gespenster stared at it for a long time out of his one good
eye, as if seeking landmarks among the crags and
pinnacles of ice which towered beyond. He pointed
silently eastward, towards the sea, and they began to
cast along the drifted snow at the base of the ice-
wall. The sun came through, bathing the landscape in
a dismal red light. Presently they stopped and, again
without speaking, the Gespenster pointed to the
tracks in the snow. Paradine stared at them, feeling
small and cold and afraid. The impressions of the
enormous pads were fresh and sharp, and ran in a
straight line from far across the plain, as if something
had come to this spot with great urgency for this
encounter, and they continued a short distance into a
broken archway in the ice-cliff.

"Buck up, lad," said the Gespenster kindly, "it's not
as bad as you think. I'll give you what help I can. It's
not much, perhaps, but it's something."

He held out an earthenware mug which Paradine
had not seen him use previously. Looking down into
it, he was not surprised to see a small dark freshet
spring up in the bottom, and the vessel filled with
dark red wine which steamed and bubbled as it
reached the brim.

"Drink it up, lad, it'll do you good."

Paradine drank if off, gasping at its heady savour;
the warmth of it seemed to run straight into his limbs.
When he lifted his head from the cup, the Gespenster
no longer towered a head over him, and the pad-
marks in the snow seemed of rather ordinary size.

He walked quickly into the ice cave. It was not dark, as he had expected, but full of a suffused and shifting red light which came from the fiery sunlight striking through the ice, but which reminded him of the heady taste of the wine. The cave widened into an inner chamber, where something huge and grey and furry watched for him with little red eyes. As he entered, it reared up on its hind legs and shambled towards him, clawed pads extended wide to grasp, cruel jaws open to crush. Wrapping his cloak about his left arm, Paradine thrust it between the beast's jaws, with his right arm he grappled it around the ribs. For a long time they struggled, and he was aware only of the dim red light and the fumes of wine in his head, the rank smell of the groaning beast and the harshness of its fur.

At last it broke away from him. He struck it on the nose with his fist, it whimpered and licked his feet. Then it scuffled towards him something which scraped and rang on the icefloor; it was a heavy bronze bowl. Picking it up, he strode from the cavern with the beast following obediently at his heels.

The Gespenster had piled snowblocks into an effective windbreak and found the means to make a fire. As Paradine approached, the tethered ponies smelt the beast and reared up, screaming with fear; but the tall man spoke to them gruffly, comforting them, and they stood still, sweating and rolling their eyes, while the beast padded past them and disappeared into the gathering dark.

"Don't worry," said Gespenster, "your pet will come back."

After their supper of boiled meal, Paradine said: "Now where do we discover the sword?"

"That's what we must find out," said his companion. He picked up the bronze bowl, and held it out to the firelight. It was dimpled with small round indentations in an apparently random pattern. Still in silence, he filled it with lumps of fresh snow, and set it close to the fire. When the snow had melted down, and the bowl was filled to the brim with the clear water, he pulled it away from the fire, and said: "Now you must feel around until your finger-tips find the right contacts—don't worry, you'll know when you've found them. And think of the sword."

Paradine knelt down by the bowl and ran his hands over the metal surface, until quite suddenly it seemed that his fingertips of their own volition found the hollows that fitted them. A rapport was established; his hands tingled and a faint resonance thrummed through the bowl, frosting the surface of the water with fine vibrations. When it cleared, a picture unblurred into sharp clarity. At first he could see nothing but a plain, white and perfectly flat; then the picture was moving, gliding over the plain towards a jumble of towers on the horizon. The movement became swifter; he was in among the towers now, floating through a blur of silent streets, until at last the picture slowed and rested in front of a tall building sheathed in green porcelain tiles. Above the wide doorway loomed the statue of a naked man, heroic and time-eroded, with outspread arms, holding in one hand a many-faceted crystal, in the other what appeared to be a conch-shell. The picture dwelt on these details as it slowly faded. Paradine looked up with a sigh.

"What did you see?" said the one-eyed man. Paradine told him, and he nodded. "The lost city on the ice," he said, "New Valdaroon. Get your sleep, lad, you'll need it. I'll watch for a while." He sat down by the fire and fed it with small twigs and pieces of broken wood; Paradine's last impression, as he sank down into exhausted sleep, was of that one implacable eye staring down into the fading embers.

The Gespenster was right about the beast; when Paradine awoke in the morning, cold, stiff and hungry, its huge grey bulk was curled up near the ashes of the fire. They loaded the ponies and set off towards the south and west, and trekked on for many days. The landscape, always fading out at the edges into grey overcast, sloped gradually upwards, becoming more broken and harder to cover. Every night the beast went off to forage on its own, and returned in the early morning, licking its bloody chops, to doze by the fire. First one baggage-pony was killed; then a second. This happened as they were crossing a barren upland, where the very ground seemed cursed by some disaster of man or nature and was no more than a dry flaky crust covered by a scurf of snow. Even the beast could find no game here; it squatted by the dying fire, eyeing them mournfully, until Paradine got up and threw it a whole haunch of the slaughtered pony. The beast devoured it, growling softly, and curled up to sleep.

They came to a country of thin ragged grass, and plodded on, foodless, leading the two remaining skinny ponies, now hardly strong enough to carry their gear, and not worth eating. The beast shambled off on some errand of his own. Even the Gespenster's gruff encouragements were silenced; only his one eye wearily scanned the murky horizon. Paradine stumbled along, leaning on the neck of his beast, drifting into sleep and watching the wraith-figures gather in the grey landscape and flicker away as he jerked his eyes open. But at dusk, when they suddenly halted, he saw in front of him a shallow valley scattered with snowflower bushes, and the bleached skeleton of a single dead tree. The ponies, unloaded, tottered off to browse on the small juicy leaves; the Gespenster tore down the rattling dead branches and struck them into a bonfire blaze; and the beast padded silently into the firelight carrying the body of a small snowdeer, which it dropped at Paradine's feet.

Next day they came out of the valley on to the frozen levels of the lake, where all was as he had seen it in the bowl. Plodding, not gliding, across the snow-covered ice-flats, they slowly drew towards the frozen city. The waters of the lake must have gradually submerged its lower levels before they froze, for the first buildings they came to were planted deep in the frozen lake, and their lower storeys could be seen stretching dimly down below in cleared patches of the ice, while the tall facades towered gaunt and empty above them. But the ice-sheet gave way to land, and the broad snow-caked street led upwards towards the green porcelain palace and the familiar portal and the strange statue-man with his prism and shell.

"In you go, lad," said the Gespenster. "Go on now, you'll be all right."

Paradine stepped through into vast dim halls, full of cases and even whole walls made of glass, many of them splintered, which had once sheltered imcomprehensible machines, now all turned to tangles of rust and disintegrating plastics. He slowly explored them until at last, in the dim depth of one that seemed to be full of the powdered remains of strange weapons, he saw a faintly glowing light, and approaching it found the sword set upright in a clean and undamaged case. It was a long, straight two-handed weapon with a plain hilt but beautifully shaped and tapered, so that even looking at it he knew it would balance well; and it glowed in the dimness with a soft green light, as if lit from within. Paradine pressed against the glass, seeking a way to open it, and at once a bell began ringing somewhere near. A door opened in the wall, and a young man stepped out. He was fair-haired and fresh-coloured, dressed in drab coveralls, and he carried a bright blade, plain but serviceable. He looked at Paradine enquiringly.

"I have come for the sword," said Paradine. "It's my quest."

"Can't allow that, I'm afraid," said the young man briskly. "No one is allowed to touch the exhibits. I'm here to see to that. I am the sword-minder. You could get into very serious trouble, you know."

"I have no quarrel with you. All I want is the sword. Let me have it and I will go away."

"Quite impossible. The orders handed down to me are very strict on this point. No touching the exhibits, they say, and especially the sword in case number XP307. That's what they say."

"It is my quest," said Paradine, "and I must take it."

The bright blade flicked up between Paradine and the glass case.

163

"If you do that, then the orders say I must kill you."

There was a deep chest-rumble in the shadows, and the grey beast suddenly reared up behind them, huge paws outspread, jaws gleaming. The young man dropped his weapon with a clatter and backed away.

"On the other hand, there's nothing in the orders to say I must get killed myself," he added. He touched a stud, the front of the case opened, and Paradine took the sword.

It not only balanced as he had expected; it was light and had a live spring to it, and seemed to fit itself to his hand. He raised it in mock salute to the young man and walked off; but soon he heard following footsteps, and, turning, found that the other was hurrying after him.

"If you don't mind," said the Swordminder, "I'll come with you. There's nothing else worth guarding anyway, and it's all rather a bore."

"Suit yourself," said Paradine, "but you'll be cold and hungry."

But the young man found strange food for them, packed in plastic and metal containers which opened with a hiss of air, and brought out a hooded fur suit for himself, which made him look bulky and tough and more like the hero of the quest-spell.

"Our way lies over the mountains," said the Gespenster as they set off again, skirting the edge of the frozen lake. "Every child knows that that is where to find the Ghost Giant and the Helm of Darkness."

So they travelled on for many days, mostly on foot now; with the beast foraging on its own as before, and the young Swordminder telling them tales of the old days to make the leagues seem shorter. The track they followed sloped upwards, among dark pine-woods and black drizzling crags wreathed in drifts of mist.

One morning as they marched on, the cliffs about them narrowed gradually into a pass. The low sun struck up from behind them, and the fog gathered in a solid bank ahead. The Gespenster, who was leading, halted and pointed ahead to where, on the ridge of the pass, a shadowy figure towered in the fog, immensely tall and squat, aureoled with faint circular rainbows. The Gespenster silently unwrapped the sword which had been carefully packed, along with the bowl, on one of the ponies, and handed it to Paradine.

"It's all yours, lad," he said comfortably. "Come along now, third time pays for all."

Comforted a little by the warm live feel of the sword's grip in his hands, Paradine advanced slowly and alone up the pass. Shimmering and vague, the immense shadow awaited him, and as he drew near, slowly raised what might have been a club made of a knotted pinetree. A puff of wind blew down the pass; the fog swirled, and the shadow bore down upon him with sudden terrifying speed. With the dense dew of the fog clinging about him Paradine wearily raised the glowing sword; the shadowy giant leaned over him and he was full of deadly cold.

There came a loud shout from the Swordminder, who had climbed up among the rocks to his right. The giant stopped and turned, wavering in the fog, with his thick legs reared up like pillars right in front of Paradine. The sword seemed to move of its own accord in one swift sweet motion, and with almost no resistance shore through the huge thighs. With a thin remote cry the ghost-giant toppled over and vanished down the slope.

Where he had stood was the gnarled stem of an old thorn tree, among the bare branches of which something glittered. Paradine reached up and pulled it down, a kind of cap made of silvery wires of various thicknesses, woven together in a seemingly random pattern. On impulse, he placed it on his head, where it settled and seemed to fit itself, with a faint tingling, to the scalp.

"Hello," called the Gespenster, striding up the path, and "Hello," called Swordminder, climbing down from the rocks. They seemed to be searching around for him, yet he stood only a few paces from them and the fog was thinning.

"Here I am," he said. Swordminder was startled, but not the Gespenster.

"So you found the Helm of Darkness," said the one-eyed man. "Take it off now, let's have a look at you."

Paradine lifted the helm. "What a splendid idea," said Swordminder, "you just seemed to materialise out of nothing. May I try it on?"

Paradine offered him the helm, but the Gespenster stopped him with a gesture.

"Not so," he said. "The Helm, like the Sword and the Bowl, will only obey one master at a time. Now press on regardless, my lucky lads, we'll be well over the pass by nightfall and then it's a straight run home."

Beyond the pass the way went steeply down, and by evening they were already among the foothills. Turning back in the evening light, Paradine saw without surprise that the tall shadowy giant was striding companionably behind them in the mists. By late afternoon of the following day, Paradine could recognise the wooded country that surrounded the city. A heavy thundershower burst overhead, and while they sheltered under a massive overhang of rock, the Gespenster carefully unpacked the bowl and put it out in the clearing. They sat together under the overhang, listening to the cheerless clatter of the downpour on the branches and to the faint ringing of the bowl in the rain.

When the storm had passed, they made a small fire and ate from their store of the tasteless preserved food. Then Paradine took the bowl, now filled almost to the brim with clear rainwater, and this time his fingers easily found their proper grips, the rapport was established and a picture formed almost at once. He was looking at the central square of the city, with the decayed elegance of the palace facade in front of him. It was dusk, but there were several fires burning on the cobbles, by the light of which he could see many people moving about. Some were dressed in robes of sombre scarlet or faded blue, the ragged and threadbare remains of noble uniforms; here and there a piece of jewellery winked in the shifting light. The

166

others were big bulky men, dressed in serviceable fur and leather and wearing helmets of dull metal. They stood or sat at ease, eating roast meat cut from the spits which turned on the fires. Shields and hand-weapons were stacked by the dry fountain; and dimly to one side, under the arcade, he could see picket-lines of horses. The big men ate and swaggered; the others in their tattered finery came and went in the light of the fires, obsequiously polite.

"Well now," said the Gespenster when Paradine had told him what he had seen, "it's not unexpected. It's a pity it had to come so soon, but perhaps it's all for the best. Those chaps in the posh clothes, they're the old city gentry. It suited them very well as long as the quest came to nothing, because it left them in charge. Happen they've heard that this time it's going to be different. And the others, well, they're the bor-derers. They've been raiding and moving this way for a long time, and now the gentlemen have invited them to come in and hold the city against all comers. There's not much to choose between them, they're a right set of villains, all of them. Now get your sleep, lads, there's work to do in the morning. We'll sort them out, don't you worry. We'll be sleeping in feather beds again tomorrow night."

And so, for the last time, Paradine lay down to sleep on the bare ground; the Swordminder snored beside him, the beast prowled in the woods, the giant was not to be seen, and the Gespenster with his one bright eye stared into the fire and fed it with small pieces of wood.

The morning mist was thick around the city as they approached it; the walls still had their patchwork look, but the gate had been put in order and a party of borderers, hunched in their furs and leaning on the butts of their broad axes, kept guard in front of it. At a nod from the Gespenster, Paradine girded on the Sword, picked up the Bowl, settled the Helm of Darkness firmly on his head, and advanced alone across the causeway. He slipped in between two of the guards and passed unnoticed up the main street and into the palace.

The dim hall with its high windows was now a crowded place. The princess sat sullenly in her high chair and a ragged throng of nobles chattered and gesticulated in front of her without order or respect. The tall bearded borderers, all heavily armed, lounged against the walls and looked on grinning.

One of the noblemen, an old hook-nosed fellow in the remains of a black velvet robe with enamelled studs and buckles, pushed forward and said roughly.

"Princess, the quests are at an end. The latest fool has been gone for a year and a day, and he will not return. We demand that you relinquish all power to a council of regency. When that is done we can ratify our agreement with our esteemed friends the borderers and arrange our affairs like reasonable men. This fairytale nonsense has gone on long enough. Sign here please." And he held out a bit of parchment and waved it at the princess, who shrank back and looked wretchedly about the crowd of snarling or grinning faces in the hall.

An invisible arm sent the old spokesman flying; a moment later the bronze Bowl dropped with a clang on the steps of the dais and Paradine appeared there, holding the glowing Sword in one hand and the glittering Helm in the other.

"The latest fool has returned," he said loudly in the astonished silence. "As you see, I bring the Bowl, the Sword and the Helm. I have fulfilled the quest. Now I claim my bride and my kingdom."

The old man scrambled to his feet and spat. "These are fakes and the man's an imposter. Guards, cut him down."

"This can easily be tested," said Paradine evenly. The sword leapt like a live thing in his hand, and the old man's head bounced across the floor. The ragged nobility turned and scrambled for the door, tangling with the burly borderers, some of whom were struggling to get at Paradine.

Behind the dais, the door in the panelling suddenly burst open and with a mad clamour the palace hounds, ugly-headed brutes, burst into the room, followed by the old herald blowing a breathless view-halloo on his trumpet.

Two of the borderers advanced confidently on Paradine, one on either side, hefting their broad axes with insolent ease. The sword whickered through the air, left and right, and two more heads rolled on the floor. The hall was filled with an insane clamour of dogs and men. The hounds, famished as always, fastened on the legs of the screaming noblemen; the borderers shouted and struck out impartially at hounds and noblemen alike.

Paradine turned to the princess who stood transformed, bright-eyed and pink-cheeked with excitement, watching the fight. He seized her, kissed her roughly and hustled her to safety through the small door in the panelling. Then he settled the Helm of Darkness on his brows, raised the Sword in both hands and went steadily down the hall, striking out rhythmically left and right like a mower. Even the borderers had had enough; trampling over the remnants of the noblemen, they thrust their way down the dusty cobwebbed corridors and out into the square.

What they saw there did not comfort them. The huge beast, its grey hair bristling with fury, rushed snarling into the square and made for the picket-lines. Screaming with terror, the horses reared and kicked and broke their halters; dashing through the borderers, they stampeded madly down the main street and out of the gate. The beast reared up on its hind legs and began batting at heads with its great paws; beside it the invisible swordsman mowed on as before.

The borderers were hardy men; those that could stand retreated in a body towards the gate, making what rearguard they could. Outside the gate, the mist was thick. As they drew back across the causeway, an enormous shadow loomed over them and seemed to strike at them with a club. They broke and ran, and most of them reeled off the causeway and foundered in the marsh.

When the noise had died away, Paradine stood on

169

the steps of the palace with the princess holding firmly to his arm. The old herald blew a wavering blast on his trumpet and sat down exhausted by the fountain. Another kind of people came creeping into the square, timidly at first, then swarming in more boldly as the news spread. They were poor and squat, dressed in rough working clothes, carrying the instruments of their trades like weapons—blacksmith's hammer, butcher's knife, thresher's flail. As they peered about, they muttered to each other, prodding the heaps of slain, fossicking for loot, trying on helmets and tattered cloaks. Their ugly faces split into wide grins; they began to laugh and caper about, clown-figures in their stolen rags and furs. Little bent women moved among them, and bandy-legged children fraternised with the palace hounds, who panted and lolled out their tongues. They all shouted "Long live Lord Paradine" and "God bless our princess Helena," and were standing around not quite sure what to do next, when the Gespenster and Swordminder rode quietly into the square on their horses and set them to work clearing up the mess and preparing for the wedding-feast. The ghost-giant had vanished with the mist; and the beast had gone off about its own business.

The next seven years were busy ones. The palace was restored to its earlier splendour of tiles and gilding; the halls and corridors were cleaned and painted, and filled with the comings and going of a business-like court. On high days there were processions and banquets, and the great hall glowed with the torches of ceremony; but at most times the palace was a place that bustled with officers and magistrates and messengers from neighbouring cities, who might be invited to eat informally with the Lord Paradine while they gave their news or took their orders, helping themselves from a table replenished by sweating cooks, and taking their ease by the crackling fire of beechlogs.

The streets were widened and many of the houses rebuilt on the old plan. The old nobility tended to hold aloof in their dark palaces; but the common people were clean and held themselves up and no longer looked ugly, and their children grew straight and tall.

The walls and gate were set in order and patrolled by a force of smart young guardsmen. The moat was cleared and the marsh drained. Every year more of the forest gave way to cornfield and pasture. One of the first things revealed to Lord Paradine by the Dream-Bowl was a long-forgotten treasure hidden in a secret room in the palace; this he used carefully to pay for public works, maintain an army and bring in craftsmen and materials from abroad.

The army, mainly light cavalry and bowmen, harried the demoralised borderers until they broke contact and disappeared. A small efficient navy patrolled the coast, and co-operated with the seagiants to destroy both pirates and seamonsters. Once more fish were plentiful in the city's market-place.

The old red sun shone quite frequently. Travellers reported that the ice-wall in the north was visibly breaking up and retreating, and that wild cattle had again appeared on the northern plains.

Seven years and a day after he had come to the throne, the Lord Paradine walked slowly through the large airy scriptorium where rows of clerks were busy over their parchments, penning despatches for the waiting couriers who idled over dice and ale in the nearby orderly room ready to set out at any moment on their fast posthorses, entering in the public ledgers records of taxation in kind, landholdings and military levies, or drawing up large public notices, for nearly everyone in the principality could now read and write. He nodded to them in greeting but did not interrupt their work.

In the raised open gallery at the end, he found Swordminder, busy as usual at his desk. He was still a cheerful modest young man, a little grey now at the temples. He had developed a great ability for supply and administration, and Paradine had made him his seneschal. All the organizing work of the principality passed across his desk, and he had slipped naturally into the position of unofficial regent during Paradine's frequent absences at the wars on land and sea or on his expeditions to the outlying provinces.

When they had dealt with the day's routine business and settled the draft plan for the new merchant-fleet, the Lord Paradine leaned back in his chair and called for wine.

"My mind often turns to the old days and to Valdaroon," he said, looking kindly at his old friend. "The hunters tell me that the ice is breaking up and that the whole city is settling slowly into the lake. I should like to go there again. There must be other treasures in your palace of green porcelain."

"There was nothing much except the sword," said Swordminder, sipping his wine. "There were marvellous things there once, but all fallen into rubbish. I hardly knew what they were. As you know, I was a wanderer in my young days, and I took refuge in Valdaroon from a storm. There was an old man there, white as winter, who kept the place. I was afraid at first, but I stayed on and he taught me what he knew, which wasn't much. Then he died, and I became the Swordminder."

"I saw strange things there," said Paradine, "great machines made of metal, and intricate small things."

"Oh, they were there," said Swordminder, "but what they were for ... " He shrugged, and then leaned forward. "There was one hall there with a high roof made of thin metal. It collapsed at last under the snow. Underneath were great machines, with wings. There were pictures of them, flying, impossible but true. There was a thing like a tall tower, all made of rusted metal, and near it were maps of the stars."

They sat silent for a while, drinking their wine and thinking of great winged shapes in the air.

"The men of old made them," said Paradine, "the city and all that was in it. Yet the ice came, and they are gone." He looked with satisfaction at the clerks busy over their desks, and the orderly racks of rolls and codices along the wall. "They are gone, and we are here, and we prosper."

"For how long?" said Swordminder, looking at Paradine over the brim of his cup. "All things have their seasons. For how long?"

"I must speak to the Gespenster about this," said Paradine rising. "I see too little of him these days. He keeps himself apart."

"One can keep too much apart. People forget," said Swordminder, "my lord."

Faintly disturbed by the sudden formal address, Paradine walked slowly out of the hall. Behind his back, Swordminder silently beckoned a courier to him.

As soon as Paradine had taken over the city, the Gespenster had set up his quarters in one of the attics of the palace—a long raftered dusty place with dormer windows which looked out across the city to the hills. There was a huge old bed and a table; the rest of the room was almost filled with a jumble of rolls and codices, some in strange letterings which Paradine had never seen before. The Gespenster passed his time there reading and dozing, or staring out of the window with his one bright eye at the broad red sun or the frosty stars, or listening to the elusive sound of the glass wind-bells which hung in a neighbouring turret. He came and went as he pleased without explanation; sometimes the room was empty for many days at a time.

As Paradine entered the room, he could hear the faint whispering chime of the bells; the massive figure stirred at the window and came to meet him. After they had talked for a while, Paradine said suddenly: "Something troubles me today. I keep thinking of Valdaroon, and the place where we found the sword. There were strange and powerful things there, all gone to rubbish. A great and powerful people must have made them, yet they are gone too, without memories."

"Not quite, lad, not quite. It's all in there—" the Gespenster nodded towards the toppling piles of written stuff—"somewhere, and I've read much of it. You are right. They were greater than anything you know. They could fly to the stars, and talk to one another from the ends of the world. But they grew

173

old, and their power shrank, and the ice crept down, so they set up that place and put all kinds of things in it, to remember by. They hoped, you see, that the good times would come again."

Paradine leaned against the sill and stared down at the orderly bustle of the market place, where the farmers had set up their rows of stalls under coloured awnings in the square, and the marshals in blue uniforms went about among the crowds to see fair trade.

"In seven years," he said, "we've done so much, and yet from up here it looks"—he turned back towards the room—"small."

"It doesn't do to worry about that, lad. A man does what he can. The past is bigger than you can know. Before Valdaroon and all it stood for, there had been other cities, and other kingdoms, and Valdaroon was to them as this to Valdaroon. The ice has been and gone many times." He ran the edge of his horny hand along the table with a harsh dry sound. "Each time it sweeps it all away—like that."

"I did not know that we could be so small," said Paradine wonderingly.

"It may be stranger than you think, lad. One of the greatest of the old kingdoms now, it is said that perhaps they had found out the last secret, that of time itself. But I can't find that in the books, and maybe it's all some old yarn. We're all carried along on the stream of time and it winds to and fro and doubles back on itself. And supposing, now, we weren't in the big stream at all, but just circling in a backwater, round and round."

His one eye seemed full of mischief and humour.

"Look, I'll show you something, and let what must happen, happen."

He rummaged about in a corner, sending several piles of manuscript toppling, before coming back to the table, holding a small volume in his hand. It was bound in some drab stuff, and when he opened it the pages were harsh and thin, quite unlike the fine smooth vellum, though the letters were incredibly small and neat.

"I'll read you what it says," he said, turning to a

174

taxes. They want to play a little, and taste the sweets of life."

"But look what I gave them," said Paradine angrily. "I lifted them out of squalor and despair. I gave them order and courage and beauty."

"The people do not really want so much," said Swordminder. "It would be a fine thing if they did. But they want so little. People have humble longings—a quiet life, an easy death. These other things embarrass them, really."

"So you've called in the borderers have you? and the old ragtag nobility, I suppose?"

"We must have stability," said Swordminder, "we've got to get back to normal. Seven years is a long time. I'm sorry, but that's how it goes. We didn't want to hurt you or the princess, really we didn't. We hoped that when you saw what had happened, you'd accept it quietly."

"The borderers would never let that happen, you know that."

"I'm sorry," said Swordminder uneasily, "but ... look, there's a pair of good horses ready at the postern gate. Take the princess and ride north. The borderers will be here in an hour. I'm glad I can do that much for you."

They remained looking at each other, and Swordminder's blade never wavered. Still rubbing his numbed fingers, Paradine turned and strode off without a word.

Within the hour, they were riding north from the city, warmly wrapped in winter furs, the horses going well under them, their hoofbeats muffled by the new snow. They pushed on until late afternoon, when they found a good posthouse and put up for the night. They gave no names, and though the innkeeper looked at them sharply, he said nothing. It was still black night when the innkeeper shook him awake out of a dead sleep.

"My lord," he whispered, the candle shaking in his hand, "my lord, I knew you and my lady, but I said nothing. Now a courier has just passed through with an escort, bating only for a sup and fresh horses. He

179

carries messages about you, my lord and lady, you are to be stopped and made captive. A flurry of borderers is riding hard behind, scouring the country for you."

He set the candle down on the table and wiped his hands on his apron. For a moment he stood there, his white lardy face sweating and working with fear, yet determined somehow to serve a last loyalty and not be wholly base.

"My lord, my lady, I have loved you for the good work you have done, but I am no warrior. There are fresh horses waiting beside the stable, and food in the saddlebags. That is all I can do."

Helena stared up from the pillow, her blue eyes strange with fear and sleep.

"Where can we go?" she whispered.

The fat innkeeper wiped his hands again and stared distractedly about the room.

"Get off the highroad as fast as you can. Listen, there is a bridge not far from the town. A league from there is one of the old tracks—they can hardly have covered that yet. Strike out along it till you reach the sea; it is cruel there at this season, but all up the coast there are summer fishing-lodges, all empty now, and you might live there through the winter."

Two days later, they saw the signal flares. First one line of black smoke trickled up into the uniform grey sky, then two more widely spaced, all behind them to the south. Two more rose slowly to their left, inland; a sixth to their right, but still behind.

"They're herding us in towards the sea," he said. "We have no choice. How do you feel? Can you still ride?"

"I can still ride," she said in a low voice. "But how long—shall we ever escape? Is there no end to this?"

"No end but one, perhaps, but there is still hope. If we can reach shelter and then the weather breaks ... One good try now, dear heart, and we'll beat them yet."

She tried to smile back at him, and followed him as he urged his horse into a steady canter. All day they went on at an even pace, and rested for the night

180

behind the broken walls of what, long ago, might have been a village. The snow still held off, but the night was damp and chill. While Helena slept wrapped in furs, Paradine dozed over a small fire, feeding it with rotted timber and drifting off into broken dreams of the good days, and of the Gespenster sitting in silent thought while the firelight glittered genially on his one eye. And at least once it seemed to him that the great hulk of the beast was there, sitting on its haunches and staring at him across the fire.

The dawn seemed long in coming and he noticed a change in the air, a smell of wet fog and sea smoke. At first light they ate frugally and rode on. He watched anxiously for signs of the coast; the horses were tiring and Helena, huddling white-faced and miserable in her saddle, could not hold out for more than another day without rest.

He could hear the sea quite near now, as well as smell it, as they rode on in the greying darkness. Suddenly the edge of the cloud on the horizon lifted like a lid and the broad rising sun shone through, flooding the landscape with red light. There was cliff-edge quite near, and beyond it the flat plain of the sea. Inland to their left, where the land rose slightly, a fog-band was steadily gathering. He reined in, staring. An immense shadowy figure was taking shape in the midst, armed and rainbowed.

"It is the ghost giant," he said wonderingly, "and last night indeed I saw the beast. They at least have come to help me."

"Do not hope too much, dear love," said Helena faintly. "This is the time when a man has no friends, neither men nor ghosts nor animals. You should have killed them all. The quest is not finished."

"Perhaps it is never finished."

With terrifying motion, the fog flowed down to catch them against the barren coast, and whirling up its shadowy weapon the giant swam swiftly through it towards them.

"Ride!" shouted Paradine, but Helena's horse gave out a scream of terror and reared up, throwing her. He leapt down beside her but as he did so his own horse screamed and jerked the rein from his hand. The fog was all about them; the great shadow seemed to stride over them; there was a drumming of hooves and a screaming from the horses, and a splashing and silence. He stayed hunched over Helena, shielding her with his body. When he lifted his head the fog had thinned away and the sun had been blotted out by cloud, leaving the bitter landscape pale and dull. The horses were gone over the cliff with their food and spare coverings; they were indeed alone.

After a little time, he rallied himself and tried to rouse Helena. She was very white and breathing shallowly; when he turned her head, there was an ugly bruise and blood clotted in the pale fair hair. She moaned when he picked her up and carried her down a dip in the track towards a small bay. There was an abandoned fisherman's hut there, four stone walls roofed with turf, and he laid her in there on a bed of dry seagrass.

With a cloth dipped in a rock-pool, he gently wiped the blood and dirt away and made a cold compress for her head. She stirred and muttered; the blue eyes fluttered open with a dazed unfocused look.

"My head is strange," she muttered, "my legs, I can't feel my legs. Where am I? my lord, where are you?"

"I'm here," said Paradine, gently taking her hand.

"He's gone on the quest," she said, "now I shan't see him, it's all got to be done again." Her head rolled painfully from side to side, and another voice came unnaturally from her mouth, like a puppet's. "All that snow," she said, "it's insane. Insane but beautiful, quite baroque." Her eyes closed again, and she murmured to herself.

For a long while he stayed there holding her hand, unmoving. Then he thought that, if there was to be any chance at all for her, he must find food. After a longish walk inland, he spotted a hare in its white winter coat, stalked it and struck it down with a pebble and a sling made from cloth torn from his

182

jerkin. He also found some edible fungi and seamoss, and with these he hurried back to make broth in the old fish-kettle left in the hut. The bleak sky was beginning to darken and the cold air seemed to be closing down on the stark landscape, fold on fold, an enormous impalpable weight.

When he crouched to enter through the low doorway, he saw in the dying light that Helena had not moved. Dropping his provisions outside, he flung himself on his knees beside her and touched her face; it was cold and stiff; there was frost on her lips and her wide blue eyes were staring open, glazed with frost. He crouched there beside her without moving; the day faded and the night wore on. The cold thickened and the sea moaned sullenly outside, lulling him into a frozen sleep.

When the cramp in his limbs woke him, he staggered outside into faint daylight and falling snow. Looking down stupidly at the ground, he saw that the body of the hare was gone and there were the tracks of large pads in the snow all about the hut. After he had slowly and painfully gathered rocks and blocked up the entrance to the hut, he began to walk out of the bay and up the grim coast, following the tracks which remained fresh and firm before him, despite the thick-falling snow. The beast was taking its time, loitering for him, leading him on. He could only follow.

The sea had changed its note, now creaking and rustling. When he looked out at it in a lifting of the snow, he saw that ice was forming along the shore, and that dim shapes and heavier masses of broken ice were drifting further out. Time had no meaning now. Presently he began to fall down and get up again and stumble on, following the fresh marks of the pads.

Abruptly the broad spoor dipped down towards the sea. The snow swirled around thicker than ever, and he was half-blind, but soon he knew by the creaking and lifting beneath his feet that he was walking on ice. There was a grumbling roar behind him which made him spin round, dimly aware that the beast had circled behind him and stood between him and the land. Its huge grey form reared up in a haze of snow and closed in, paws spread out for the killing blow.

"At least I have a little of my old strength," he thought, and laughed. "Gespenster, where is your wine?"

Then the grey bulk rushed down upon him like a cloud; its carrion breath blew in his face and he scrabbled with numb hands at the harsh fur. As the great jaws swung at him, his feet slipped on the ice and the fangs closed rendingly in his left arm and side, crushing him down into pain and darkness.

In a dream or out of a dream, he lay by the edge of the sea-ice, his body seared by the pain of the cold in his wound. Something splashed and snorted. The kindly stupid face rose tall out of the water beside him, and the seagiant stared down at him with his little eyes and gently blew steamy breath from slitted nostrils.

"Poor mathter, nithe mathter," it boomed softly, "lie thtill, theaman take mathter to kind fwiend, make mathter better." The huge cold leathery hands slid underneath and raised him; cradled in them, he was carried gently out into the sea of darkness.

The seagiant dressed his grievous wound and carried him across the dark water to the ship were the Gespenster waited for him. The past fell away and his body healed. They came to the city and Paradine undertook the quest. In the ice cavern, he tamed the Beast and redeemed the Bowl; in the lost city, he mastered Swordminder and resumed the Sword; in the mountains, he conquered the Giant and found the Helm.

Returning victorious to the city, he overthrew the nobility and drove out the borderers, married the princess and set the kingdom in order. For seven years and a day, there was peace and plenty in the land. Then the Gespenster showed him the book and left him; the bowl, the sword and the helm failed him; Swordminder, the giant and the beast turned against him. Driven into the wilderness with Helena

184

dead, he lay torn and bloody on the ice until the seagiant came for him.

He was healed by the Gespenster and undertook the quest and returned victorious and set the kingdom in order and was betrayed and driven out and Helena died and he lay torn and bloody on the ice.

He returned and quested and triumphed and governed and was betrayed and lay on the ice.

He rose, he fell. From the sea to the sea, from the ice to the ice.

The cycles spun faster and smaller. Winding in and in, faster and faster, the gyres tightened in a decreasing spiral which drove down to meet its vanishing point in the floor of darkness.

TEN

EVERYTHING AND NOTHING had both happened and not happened; time was as broad as it was long; space was neither here nor there; the loop of eternity threaded itself through the eye of zero.

It was a landscape of old newspapers; he could see that much in the glaucous light of the stars which moved visibly in random patterns. At first sight there seemed to be nothing else. As he moved about he sank up to his knees and floundered along in the newspapers, which made a dry whispering and rustling sound about him, like the leaves of the world-tree drifted down on the floor of some last forest beyond the end of the world. Every so often a wind blew drearily from between the irregular stars and sent sheets of paper scampering along or raised them in swirling flocks high into the air, where they fluttered about and slowly settled again.

Presently he found that there were other objects scattered here and there, buried among the papers. First there was a pile of chairs, half-submerged, and an enormous coffin, and what proved to be a stuffed rhinoceros. Later he found a small sick tree with one leaf on it, a pile of manure and a couple of old dustbins; as he watched them the lids stirred as if there was something inside, but a gust of starwind buried them again in newspapers.

He never did find out all the many kinds of things that lay buried among the perpetually whispering, stirring, shuffling newspapers. There was an old-time motor car, one of the internal-combustion type, and a good deal of cast-off clothing which smelt musty, and huge unidentifiable bones, and a thing made of steel wire which might have been some kind of harp, and several old rocket-tubes.

As he trudged slowly about in the yielding surface, the random gusts of starwind stirred the papers perpetually, sometimes far off where they looked like drifting snowflakes, sometimes close by, so that they sailed and fluttered around him like a storm of birds.

After a long time, or so it seemed, he came upon an antique bedstead made of tarnished brass, and he began to sweep the drifted newspapers off it, thinking that it might give him a place to rest. But it was already occupied. Helena lay there, small and shrunked, dressed in rags, with swollen belly and peastick limbs like the body of a starved child, her face and staring eyes thickly glazed over with frost.

Spinning about, he ran and plunged and floundered through the maddening papers until he fell down exhausted and, after a fashion, slept. The paper leaves of the world-tree drifted down and covered him from the shifting stars and the inconsequent wind that blew between them.

He awoke shivering with cold. The wind was blowing the papers about in a grey storm, and fluttering the tatters of his uniform. He hunched forward and stared out over the meaningless landscape. If I hadn't lost my glowlighter, he thought, I could set fire to the bloody place; the thought of all this paper blazing and blowing away in a storm of fire filled him with sudden glory. But the lighter was lost, gone somewhere with the rest of his gear. I must try to live, he thought, somehow, and he trudged off through the drifts of paper, a clownish figure in his rags.

Presently he found another of the abandoned vehicles, an old cargo-machine this time. He forced open the doors and crawled inside; it was full of broken cases, their contents spilled about the floor. Much of it was spoilt, but there were food canisters still intact, and opening one of them with the key provided, he found that it contained some kind of pulpy pink fruit preserved in syrup. I'm hungry, he thought with surprise, I'm thirsty, and sitting down on a case he ate the fruit with his fingers and slowly sucked up the juice.

At first he thought vaguely of stories that he had read or seen on tape or video, of shipmen wrecked on islands and spacemen wrecked on asteroids, and of all the brave and ingenious things they had done in order to survive. He would find and drag together other old vehicles to make a platform and stockade in the shifting welter of newspapers; then he must salvage and stockpile enough containers of food and liquid for survival. In time he might find some way of detecting and communicating with other life-forms. He must not let himself slip into a state of sensory deprivation, a final autism. I am a man, he thought, and men survive. I must keep a calendar, re-establish my hold on time. Then he looked up at the erratic movements of the faint stars, and knew that there was nothing by which he could take hold on anything.

He stared out of the back of the vehicle at the scuttering newspapers, catching meaningless flashes of headlines. MULTICOON KRAAG LOST IN UNSPACE (they said)—ART DEAD, PROF CLAIMS—STOCKMART MEGA-CRASH, FTOOMIANS WIPED—KRAAG SUPERWEAPON THREAT—PLAYBOY SCANDAL CRASH PROBE—ARE VALD-AROON RELICS OLDY FAKES?—TRUTH ONE AND MANY STATES ORACLE—ICE AGE LATEST—COSMIC INSTABILITY WARNING—ANDROID PAY STRIKE—MILLENNIUM DECLARED: OFFICIAL—SUN GOES NOVA.

A gust of wind scattered them high into the air, uncovering something which looked like a white stone, bedded among papers. Paradine scrambled from the store vehicle and picked it up. It was a plaster mask of a human face, with strong broad brow, flat nose, heavy jaw, empty eyes and mouth. As he held it up before him at arms' length, its sudden strange humanity overwhelmed him; with its calm noble look, it took into itself all the friendships, all the stray contacts, all the ugly, perverse, humorous or interesting faces of his short life. He wanted to weep for joy and to laugh with sorrow. Hurriedly, breathlessly, he laid it in the back of the van, and scrabbled about in the accumulated rubbish for corroded metal rods, rolls of newspaper, scraps of wire. When he had fumbled all this together into the rough shape of a human figure, he planted it upright among the drifted newspapers and carefully bound the mask on the top. Now at last he could squat and stare at his companion.

Then a gust of starwind blew down through the void mouth of the mask, and it was the voice of Jesus saying: *The kingdom of God is within you.* He thought about this for a long while before he understood it. Then slowly, cautiously, he took it all into his mind, the wilderness of rubbish, the futile wasted stars, and the shrunken body of Helena lying in the big bedstead under its mask of frost. When it was all inside his mind at last, he began to sort it out and take it apart; it took some time (if one could call it that) to unpick it all so patiently like a thrifty woman unravelling an old woollen sock and winding it off. But at last he had it all broken down into molecules, the molecules into their constituent elementary atoms, the atoms into their component protons, neutrons, positrons, pions, muons, electrons, antiprotons, strange particles and so forth. These in turn he sorted out into their triplets of constituent quarks. Only the mask remained unassimilated.

He waited. A second gust blew through the hollow eyes of the mask, and it was the voice of Plotinus saying: *The eye could not behold the sun if its essence were not formed like the sun.* When he had contemplated on this, he began with growing confidence to rebuild. He reassembled the simple basic hydrogen and helium and watched them in his mind forming, drifting, spinning in the enormous dust-clouds of the protogalaxies. Gradually these spangled and sparkled with all the colours of the stars, main sequence, red giant, white dwarf, supernova, star cluster. He watched them glittering in their webs of light like coloured sequins in skeins of pale wool.

A third gust blew through the flaring nostrils of the mask, and it was the voice of Blake saying: *Eternity is in love with the productions of time.* Then the mask crumbled and was assimilated, and it was all within him. He focused down onto one particular galaxy, a misty wheel of light which he allowed to swing slowly past in the majestic round of the Great

189

Year. He must find a star within the right range, G-type for preference, and catch it at the precise moment of galactic time when it was beginning to throw off its broad roiling ring of gases and heavy elements, and take hold of one of the more moderate planets inside the zone of the gas-giants, and see what he could do with it. Since this needed fine workmanship, he was prepared to be patient and have many failures.

The first one he tried turned out to be a water-world, and he abandoned it to an eternity of empty seas. In the second he over-compensated and found himself with nothing but dry wind and rock. So he went on, balancing, adjusting, refining, until he knew that he had the right basic formula.

He braced himself for the next step, the making of life. At his first attempt, he worked without difficulty up to protein-chains before he became tired and abandoned it, a pleasant little tropical planet with an ocean of warm soup. Then he rested for a time and a space, sorting out possibilities. There were many attempts after that, all of them somehow wrong, a world of slow, mindless photosynthesisers, a world of sightless burrowers, a tree world full of birds, and so on.

Immense weariness grew on him and he longed at last to be home. He could feel his energy bleeding away into the stream of time. There could not be many more tries, perhaps only one, as the starry wheel spun before him. Throwing all his knowledge and all his longing into this last effort, he improvised like a master, adjusting, elaborating, here drawing in broad strong lines, there extemporising an airy fantasy, working with excruciating love and care over some cherished detail, until at last, on the edge of exhaustion, utterly drained of power, he knew that what he had made was, more or less, satisfactory.

It was escaping from him now, no longer under his control. He let it go gladly, thus becoming himself a part of it. He was drifting down out of the stark immensities into zones of golden and blue air, down through winds and clouds towards the green planet.

190

Below there, he knew, were such things as giraffes and honeybees, and troutstreams flowing clear below snowy mountains, and breadfruit sweetpotatoes and strawberries, peacocks and rhododendrons and merino sheep and a watermill.

He was walking along a narrow path beside a lake. A cloud of waterbirds flew up crying around him, and he saw Helena standing there, a blue-eyed sunburnt woman with her skirts kilted up above her knees and her strong legs planted in the shallow water, as she cut basket-rushes with a small sickle. She smiled and waved when he came towards her. Together they bundled up the rushes; he swung the bundle lightly onto his shoulder, and they walked off arm in arm along the path beside the lake.

Behind them, in the blue sky, the thunder rumbled to itself: "Increase and multiply, my children, and replenish the earth."

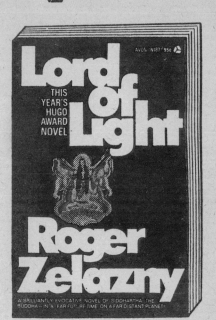